DODGED A BULLET

A SAMANTHA TRUE MYSTERY
BOOK 6

KRISTI ROSE

BOOKS BY KRISTI ROSE

<u>Samantha True Mysteries- Laugh out loud twisty mysteries</u>

One Hit Wonder

All Bets Are Off

Best Laid Plans

Caught Off Guard

Two Time Loser

Dodged A Bullet

<u>A Cold Case Mystery Series:</u>

Bone of Contention (Free at Prolific Works until October 2023)

<u>A Liars Island Suspense (written under pen name Robbie Peale)</u>

Perfect Place

<u>Campus Murder Club-Coming Soon</u>

Campus Murder Club

<u>The Wyoming Matchmaker Series- Whether marriage of convenience or star crossed lovers, everyone earns their happily ever after in this series.</u>

The Cowboy Takes A Bride

The Cowboy's Make Believe Bride

The Cowboy's Runaway Bride

Love Comes Home

CHAPTER ONE

Toby Wagonknecht placed two coffee mugs on the table before taking a seat across from me.

"We need an office," he said as he dropped three sugar cubes into his coffee.

What he meant was *he* needed an office. As my IT guy, he was the one who had equipment that needed electricity. I could store my stuff: scanners, mini cameras, and trackers, on a shelf in my closet.

"We can't afford an office," I replied.

"But work has been pretty steady for us."

I nodded. "It has, but insurance work isn't the best paying gig for a private investigator. It's a steady gig, and I like steady. Besides, if we were to get an office, even a co-share situation, you and I would have to take a big pay cut to cover the office cost. And I can't see either of us wanting to do that."

Toby reared back as if the words had horrified him. "How big?"

"Huge," I said. Yeah, I was exaggerating, sorta. But for

the first time in a lot of years, I had money in the bank. A real life, honest-to-God savings account with a healthy balance. And I wanted to keep it that way.

Opening up a PI base of operations *would* be great, but the expense wouldn't. "So, for now, we meet clients here or other places. Besides, what's wrong with Lark's coffee shop? Most Tuesday morning's people find themselves stuck in a cubicle, and we aren't." I looked around the place. Lark had recently redone the interior. "What's she calling this place these days?"

"The Steamy Cup, I think." Toby dropped another cube in his coffee. "I like these sugar cubes." He tossed one in his mouth and wagged his brows.

"I wonder how many people have touched that cube?" My question was part genuine curiosity and part messing with his head for fun.

His face froze briefly, then a few muscles twitched as he likely considered my words. Finally, he met my gaze and shrugged. "I've been shot. What can be worse than that?"

I rolled my eyes, then glanced at my watch. "They should be here any time now."

"What if the lack of privacy kills this deal?"

I shrugged, my reaction opposite of the worry I had about that exact issue. "What if the lack of privacy makes them feel safer? Maybe the casual setting will help with easing anxiety. I'm banking on that."

The entry door swung open, the bell Lark had installed above it emitting a happy chime.

"Welcome to The Steamy Cup," Lark yelled happily from behind the counter.

Her shop's previous theme had been about a person's aura and her suggestions on what they should drink to cleanse it. That theme had gone over like a lead balloon. Especially for me. When a girl marries a guy who turns out to have lied about his identity, happens to already be married to someone else, and is trying to run a scam in said girl's hometown, it doesn't take a genius to know my aura was jacked up. And a mere year of time passing did nothing to abate the strong emotions I felt about my past. Emotions that make me want to use my stun gun on someone until the charge is dead.

I stood and gave a small wave. Two dark-haired women had entered. They looked to be in their early twenties. Dressed casually in jeans and T-shirts, though one had a sweater vest on over her tee. They weren't twins, or even related, according to my research. But they looked like they could be.

"Lora?"

The one without the sweater vest nodded. She pointed to her friend. "This is Vanessa."

Toby stood, his mouth slack and catching flies. I shoved him in the shoulder.

"This is my associate, Toby Wagonknecht. He does all my IT. That's why I asked him to join us."

Toby, lanky and rail-thin, stood ram-rod straight and pushed back his shoulders. "I'm a huge fan. I subscribe to your YouTube channel. It... It's such a pleasure to meet you both." He stuck out his hand.

Lora smiled. "You game? What's your favorite?" She shook Toby's hand. He pumped hers vigorously.

"I love Zelda. That's my go-to. I wasn't a fan of *Shadowland Walker* until I started watching your videos, and then I got into it."

In our research, Toby had told me that Lora Darling and

Vanessa Taylor had started a YouTube channel when they were in high school, five years ago. Lora, the older sibling to twin brothers used the channel as a way to help her brothers learn the ins and outs of various games. She'd been asked by her parents to make sure the games her brothers wanted to play were age appropriate. She and Vanessa had turned that task into a multimillion-dollar business. Today, they were known as the gamers who were the most kid friendly and were trusted by parents. Though over the years, Lora had become the face of the channel as Vanessa had put her energy into college. She'd just graduated with a business degree.

I gestured to our table. "Have a seat."

Toby twitched with excitement. In a breathless rush, he said, "Can I get you drinks?" He gestured to the large menu on the wall over the counter. "Lora, I know you like boba, but they don't have that here, but they do have these little bad boys if you like sugar in your coffee." He pushed the sugar-cube bowl toward them. "Like a burst of energy in every bite. I know it's not the same, but it kinda is." He tossed one in his mouth and chewed like a rabbit munching lettuce. He opened his mouth to continue his ramble, but Vanessa cut him off.

"We'll get drinks and be right back." She smiled widely at Toby and patted his arm. Then the two headed off to the counter.

I steered Toby to a chair. "Take a deep breath, and stop eating the sugar cubes."

"I got all fanboy, didn't I?" His already ghostly white skin was two shades paler. "How bad was it?"

"You don't want to know. Good thing you've got Lady M," I winked. "You're fine." Lady M or Lady Marmalade was a sugar glider and Toby's emotional support animal. He'd gotten her after he'd been shot.

Subconsciously, he reached for his chest where Lady M typically was housed in a pouch shaped like an orange. He glanced over his shoulder to where Lora and Vanessa were getting their drinks. "Don't let me talk when they come back."

I chuckled. A moment later the two friends rejoined us at the table.

Lora looked around the empty coffeeshop, then met my eyes and smiled. "This place is nice. Why is it so empty?"

I shrugged. "Maybe time of day?" It was between breakfast and lunch. But what I didn't add was that Lark and her aura reading had put off a fair amount of the locals.

Vanessa blew on her drink before saying, "We just bought a house in Wind River a few months ago and haven't explored the downtown. We've been stupid busy."

Lora yawned. "Stupid busy. We're on the cusp of landing a big sponsorship deal with a popular kids' streaming service, and they've been having us go to various screenings and such to field-test us."

Vanessa added, "Make sure we have the following we say we do." She rolled her eyes. "If it wasn't such a great deal, I'd insist we walk away from it."

Lora grinned. "But it's a great deal. So, we do all the travel and waving at the camera and smiling while trying to find content for our channel. Who knew making a few videos for my brothers would have led to this."

Vanessa pointed to Lora. "She does all the waving and smiling. I'm behind the scenes now with the business side, and it's a lot better than being in front of the camera."

"We shouldn't complain, we've got all we could ever

we have, the problem we want your help with, is that the PI we used thinks he identified the stalker."

Lora interjected, "But we think he's wrong, and he won't listen to us. He insists that the emails and gifts are coming from a guy named Caleb Harris. But we know Caleb; he's harmless. Yes, he's sent some weird emails. He's kinda odd, but he's really harmless."

I cleared my throat. "Are you one hundred percent sure the stuff came from Caleb?"

They looked at each other again, then Lora shrugged. "Our PI is. I guess we aren't. I just can't see Caleb wanting to hurt me."

I didn't say that their mentality was part of why issues with the stalker had gone on as long as they had. Denial. Disbelief. Ted Bundy worked a rape hotline. The BTK killer went to church and ran a Boy Scout troop. I married a married man. Just because you can't imagine a person being capable doesn't mean a person isn't capable of bad things.

Lora continued. "But the PI wants me to file a restraining order. He wants to build a case to get Caleb put in jail. Our PI is very aggressive about the situation, and it's stressing me out." She rubbed her stomach.

Vanessa cleared her throat. "It's affecting everyone. The letters are scary enough, but the PI's response is just making our stress skyrocket at the office, and since the office is our home, we can't seem to get away from it."

Lora rubbed her stomach some more. "Moving into the big leagues was stressful, but these letters ... these gifts, are creepy, and Walt—that's the PI—is so confrontational, I've developed a stomach ulcer."

"And you want me to do what?" I liked the friends, but I wasn't sure what, specifically, they wanted from me. Yeah, their PI was aggressive, but I couldn't fault him for that. Stalker cases were notoriously underhanded, and often the consequences were devastating. I couldn't say I wouldn't react the same way for a client.

"We want you to prove Caleb isn't the stalker. Walt gave us one week to prove Caleb's innocence." Vanessa laughed. "I don't know how he thinks we're supposed to do that, and we know by asking you to prove Caleb is innocent means there's still someone out there who is stalking Lora. We'll cross that bridge after we get Caleb off the hook."

Lora interjected, "But you can't tell our staff that you're a PI. We can't handle the confrontation it'll cause. We know that's asking a lot, but if you could do this ... you know ... undercover like ... we'd appreciate that. I mean, if Walt knows we're hiring another PI, things will get so ugly." She pressed her stomach harder and rolled her shoulders inward, like she was trying to minimize the pain.

"My mom hired him. It would make things tense there too. She still sees us as kids who don't have the life experience to make solid decisions." Vanessa rolled her eyes. "We know we're asking a lot, but we're willing to pay for it."

"And there's a bonus too if you can do this soon. Walt gave us a week. We would love to make this all go away ASAP," Lora said.

Taking this case, with clients of this stature was a boon in and of itself. But a bonus would go a long way to secure my company's future even more. I glanced at Toby. A slight nod from him told me he thought we could do it.

"Okay," I said. "I'll take the case." This guy could be innocent or guilty, but I was going to find the truth and present it, regardless. And if he was guilty like the PI said, then maybe the two friends would hear my case against Caleb and take action.

Stalker cases were tricky. Yet I had a personal interest in these types of cases. In protecting people. And their PI had done a lot of the legwork for me. Should be quick and easy to wrap up.

CHAPTER TWO

Precious finished with my French braid then twirled me around to give me an inspection. Dark skirt, crisp white button-down, professional flats. She nodded in approval, then handed me my messenger bag, which I hung across my body.

We'd been best friends since grade school when Precious had been pulled out from class because she stuttered, and I had been pulled out because I couldn't read. That commonality had made us fast friends, a group that also included Hue Stillman, the younger brother to my current boyfriend and Wind River's premier detective, Leo Stillman.

My boyfriend. Weird how that didn't roll off the tongue. I mean Leo and I hadn't gotten along for well, most our lives … but lately, we were getting along just fine. Just fine indeed.

Precious, real name Erika, though no one ever called her that, straightened my collar. "I think you'll pass." She scanned me up and down.

"Thanks for giving up your Wednesday morning gym time to help me."

She gave me a thumbs-up and a smile. "You'll need one of these." She handed me a coach's whistle on a long lanyard.

I took the whistle with trepidation.

"It's for looks. You won't have to actually blow it or anything. Unless you're being chased by someone, and then the whistle could come in handy."

We grinned at each other. Because for most people, getting chased by someone was not likely going to happen. My world was different. "Are you sure you're okay with me posing as one of your assistants? I don't want to drag you into this. What if something goes wrong?" I asked.

"Do you think something will go wrong?"

I shook my head. "But we never know. For all intents and purposes, this should go smoothly. The other PI has done a lot of the work. Lora delivered his file over to me yesterday, and I've started going through it. All I have to do is find another plausible explanation for his evidence. Once Toby has remote access to Lora and Vanessa's computer, then we should be able to do some tracking and prove Caleb isn't the stalker. Maybe even nail down the person behind all of this. If it's truly not Caleb."

"What are the odds?"

I shrugged. "Unless this PI is an idiot, it's unlikely this guy is innocent, and if that's what I find, that's what I share. And so long as I don't have to do any real-life coaching, pretending to be your assistant should be fine. But..."

"Life Coach Lesson One; there is no room for buts. 'But' means you are already anticipating things going south, and many people believe that's a self-fulfilling prophecy."

This summed up Precious and I to a *T*. She was an optimist. I was a pessimist. Even in a situation such as the one we were in, a situation where I've considered every contingency, I still thought something could go wrong.

Precious cleared her throat. "Just stay positive. I'll be in your ear coaching you. No worries."

Toby handed me a flesh-colored earpiece also called an earwig. The small device would provide two-way communication. I inserted it, and Precious used a tendril of hair to mask it. The two-way communication system was the first real purchase I'd made for my business. Well, that and a tracker. I hadn't used the tracker yet, afraid I'd put it on a car and never see it again. I didn't have money to throw away, so a person had to be worthy to get the tracker on their car.

Toby patted my shoulder. "We'll be in a car down the road listening and chiming in if you need us. Once you insert the thumb drive into Lora and Vanessa's computer, it'll take maybe two minutes for me to have remote access."

I nodded. The goal was to meet the staff including the PI, get access to the computers, and establish myself as a presence they'd need to get used to seeing around.

"Okay," I said. "Let's get the show on the road."

I drove my old Wagoneer, affectionally named LC after Lewis and Clark because we'd had many adventures together, to the new subdivision in downtown Wind River. Many of the houses had water views and steep price tags. Precious and Toby followed in Precious's SUV. They parked down the street. I parked at the curb in front of the house, since another car was in the drive, its trunk popped open.

I made my way up the drive. Lason Dell, my boss at the Click and Shop, stepped out of the garage. His eyes went wide when he saw me.

Oh crap!

Lason knew I was a PI and that I filled in the dry spells

by working for his grocery as a shopper for online customers. Only I hadn't done that in a few months as my PI work had been steadily picking up.

He could blow my cover.

He was also one of the nicest people I knew, and he'd hate to learn he maybe said something he shouldn't.

"Hey, Sam," he said. He looked over his shoulder then back at me again, scanning my outfit. I could see the wheels spinning in his head.

"Hi. Lason. What brings you here? I didn't know you were working the delivery side?"

He stopped at his trunk and nodded. "Short-staffed, and I like getting out of the store. You?"

I gestured to where Lora and another woman in her early twenties were standing in the garage. Lora gave a wave.

"Miss Darling hired Erika Shurmann as her life coach. I'm an assistant to Ms. Shurmann." I gave a toothy, maniacal grin and met his gaze, raising my brows slightly so he'd hopefully get the message that I was there for reasons other than what I'd said.

Lason registered the information and gave a short, clipped nod. "Well, I'm almost done, and I'll be out of your way. It was good seeing you."

"You too. Here, let me help." I reached in and grabbed three large cartons of mochi ice cream. I followed Lason into the garage.

To Lora I said, "I used to work for Lason, before I started working for Ms. Shurmann." I gestured to the ice cream balls. "Someone is a fan of these."

Lora grinned. "Me, I have this ritual: boba tea and mochi when I'm competing. Comfort food to help with the anxiety."

"Though they're not the best for her ulcer," the other woman said. "Hi, I'm Addie Milner. I'm Lora and Nessa's assistant. You're the life coach?"

"Assistant to the life coach. I'm Samantha," I said. "I'd take your hand but..." I nodded to the boxes in my arms.

Addie jumped. "Oh, sorry, they go in here." She gestured to a door that opened to the house and then scurried to the doorway. "The freezer is right in here."

I followed and stepped inside the house. Lason was in there stacking items in the freezer. He took the boxes. The upright freezer was very organized and filled with pizza rolls, taquitos, ice cream, and now, mochi. Food for the bachelor lifestyle, or bachelorette in this case.

Lason finished stacking the items in the freezer. He dusted his hands on his pants. "That's it. Anything else I can do for you?"

Addie shook her head. She was the complete opposite of Lora and Nessa. Light to their dark. A short, ear-length blonde bob, expressive hazel eyes. She handed Lason some rolled bills. "Thanks for organizing the freezer for me. One less thing I have to do today."

Addie had a friendly smile. The kind that made a person smile in return, which Lason and I did. Lason nodded to me, then stepped out of the house.

Lora came in and closed the door. The three of us stood in what had to be the butler's pantry. Beside the upright freezer there were cabinets and shelves with the standard appliances on them. Blender, Instant Pot, toaster.

Lora said, "Okay, Nessa is in the office. Walt and Nessa's mom, Catherine Siegel, are here as well."

In my ear, Precious said, "Does the mom come a lot? Hard to grow up if your mom is hovering."

To Lora I asked, "Does Nessa's mom come here a lot?"

Addie snorted, then ducked her head. Pink stained her cheeks.

Lora rolled her eyes. "Yeah, you could say that. When Nessa announced we were in the running for a sponsorship from that kids' streaming service, Catherine started coming around a lot more."

"She used to be an actress," Addie said. "She loves all things related to that industry."

I nodded in understanding. The ringing of a phone broke the brief silence.

"That's me," Addie said and hustled off.

Lora faced me. "We still have a land line, as this area has spotty cell service."

Toby and I had done a cursory search of the employees and family before taking the case. Catherine Siegel had married a producer with a decent filmography, Brice Taylor. Catherine herself had been in a few slasher movies, though many of her parts had been roles such as lady walking by or customer in the store. Nessa had been only a year old when Brice Taylor had left Catherine for a younger, newer model. He was currently on his fifth wife. Catherine had never remarried.

"Guess it's time to meet everyone. Ready?" I asked Lora.

She bit her lip and nodded. "Walt has already started harping about filing a restraining order against Caleb. If this place wasn't also my home, I'd leave, but I can't. Besides, I need to prep for the competition Thursday, and he's making my stomach hurt."

"Let's see if I can help with that." I nodded toward the door that led to the rest of the house. "Lead the way."

Lora led me through a kitchen and living room to an

office in the front of the house. One side of the downstairs appeared to be designated for the business. Nessa had an office with a door; the dining room appeared to be Addie's space. A lovely glass desk with built-in shelves made up her office. Across the hall from Nessa's office, a larger room looked like it might have been a formal living room but was now gaming space. Two desks with multiple monitors, cameras, circle lights, and mics filled the area.

"This is my office," Lora said with a grin and flicked a bobblehead on her desk. She gestured for me to go into Nessa's office.

Slumped in her office chair was Nessa. She looked exhausted. An older woman with long blonde perfect curls and bright lipstick sat in a chair across from Nessa. Her arms were crossed over her chest as she frowned.

An older man, thinner and taller than I expected, stood over Nessa's desk, leaning toward her in what felt like an aggressive manner to me. The air in the room was thick with discomfort.

"Excuse me," Lora said. "I wanted to introduce you all to Samantha. She's my life-coach's assistant."

I smiled and waved. Only Nessa returned the gesture.

"Whoa," I said. "Did we interrupt something? Because the air in here is thick. Tense." I reached into my messenger bag and pulled out a tiny can of scented vanilla room spray. I pumped the nozzle a few times, scattering a mist around the room. "Everyone needs to just take a deep breath and calm down. Sir, you look very tense. Why don't you take a seat." I gestured to the chair. I was totally improvising.

"Who are you again?" Walt Anders narrowed his eyes at me.

"I'm the person here to help Lora with managing all the

changes that are coming her way and to make sure her health doesn't get worse. The atmosphere in here isn't helping." I turned to Lora. "If this is what your workday has been like, I now see why you needed Ms. Shurmann." I whipped out a notebook. "I'm going to make note of this." I made random scribbles on the page in the notebook, then slapped it closed. "Now, everyone. Let's take a deep breath." I put my hand to my chest. "Deep breath in through the nose like this." I sucked in a long breath through my nose.

"I do not sound like that," Precious said in my ear.

I channeled my yoga instructor. "Feel your chest moving out, then in. Deep breath." It took a lot for me not to laugh.

"Oh, for Pete's sake." Walt slapped his hand on the desk. "We'll talk about this later." He stormed out.

Behind him I yelled, "Later is good. You'll have a chance to calm down."

He grumbled something I couldn't make out.

Catherine Siegel stood. "This is very serious business, this stalker. And you girls don't seem to be taking it seriously at all." She gave me a pointed look. "Scented spray is not going to fix this." She faced her daughter. "I couldn't imagine anything happening to you, so you must understand why I'm so persistent. You're my child. It's my job to make sure you're safe."

"Yes, Mom, I know. It's just that Lora and I don't think Caleb is dangerous, and I'm not convinced he's the stalker. I'd feel more comfortable if there was more evidence before we take such formal legal actions."

Catherine pointed to a sheet of paper on Nessa's desk. "Not dangerous? How can you say that? The things he's threatened to do to Lora would make me want to hide away forever. I wouldn't feel safe here. I wouldn't feel safe at any of those red-carpet events that are planned. I wouldn't feel safe anywhere." She said the last part to Lora.

"Mom, that's not helpful," Nessa said.

Catherine threw up her hands and stalked out. Nessa got up and closed the door behind her.

Lora sank into a chair.

I dug into the messenger bag and pulled out the thumb drive. "Plug this in, and Toby can get started. We'll do your computers next, Lora. In the meantime, I'll stay the day and run interference."

"Thank God," Nessa collapsed in her chair, taking the thumb drive and plugging it into her desktop computer.

"I have my laptop right here." Lora tapped a laptop sitting on Nessa's desk with her toe. Beside it was the print out Catherine had pointed to. I picked it up and read it. It was an email to Lora.

I gave a low whistle. "When did this come?"

"Today." Lora said quietly.

"Toby," I said.

"Yeah," his voice came through the earwig.

"Email dated today at three a.m. The sender wrote, and I quote, 'I want you to die.' Let's get on this now. Trace the IP if you can."

"Got it," he said.

To Lora and Nessa, I said, "This is a threat on your life. You need to bring in the police."

CHAPTER THREE

THE NEXT AFTERNOON I MADE MY WAY TO LORA AND Nessa's. I'd spent the morning with Toby going through their emails and digging more into the lives of Nessa, Lora, and anyone connected to them. For the most part, everyone was coming out clean. The PI, Walt, had a successful business and a fair number of one-and-two-star reviews, but that was to be expected. None of the reviews were red flags.

I arrived at the house, and following a text from Lora, used a five-digit code at the front door to unlock it. I entered the foyer with Lora and Nessa's offices on each side. Two diffusers pumped out an aroma that made me want to go to Hawaii and drink a piña colada. The lights were low, ambient. The glow from Lora's computer cast shadows. Yet the vibe at Nessa and Lora's house was certainly not chill, regardless of all the attempts they had made. The energy was off. The aroma felt forced and canned. Something had soured the air. Likely a recent spat.

I went into the kitchen where Lora and Nessa stood on one side of the island and Walt and Catherine on the other.

"We aren't canceling our participation." Nessa crossed her arms, her expression hard. "To do so doesn't make sense. The threat yesterday didn't say anything about the competition today, so I don't see how they're connected."

Walt sighed. "It's the visibility. We think right now Lora needs to lie low. Get out of the spotlight a little."

Nessa rolled her eyes. "The spotlight is our job. We have a real chance at this sponsorship, and competing in the game tonight is too important of an opportunity. Lora needs to be gaming tonight."

Catherine said, "But Lora isn't the only face of the company, Vanessa. And the followers love you too. I'm sure the sponsors would as well."

Nessa shook her head. "So it's okay for me to be seen but not Lora? I don't get that."

Walt rested his palms on the island. "I'd prefer neither of you be seen, but if we reduce Lora's exposure a little, this stalker might settle down some, and you'll get that extra time you've been asking for — if you're so sure it's not Caleb. Of course, it'll give me more time to prove it is." He faced Lora. "I can't protect you online, Lora."

With the girl's permission, I'd shown the letter to Leo, and he'd given his input, but truthfully, Toby and I were already doing what he'd advised.

Lora nodded. "I know that. Online bad behavior is something I expect and I'm used to. So long as we're safe here at home, then I'm not going to worry about online. Sadly, doxing and swatting and trolling are all things I expect."

"I walked the perimeter and checked all the entry points. The house is safe. For now. But that doesn't mean Caleb won't show up."

"It's not Caleb," Nessa insisted.

Catherine slapped her hand on the counter. "Vanessa—"

I stepped into the room and cleared my throat. "Sorry to interrupt." I glanced at my watch. "The game starts in an hour. I think we should spend some quiet time getting our heads in the right place." I was totally making this up on the fly but knew Nessa and Lora needed an exit.

Addie burst into the kitchen from the garage. "Boba tea has arrived. Sorry I'm late. Traffic was backed up." In her hand she held two drink carriers. Three tall cups sat in one carrier and four in another. She bustled to the island and slid the carriers across the surface.

Nessa grabbed one and offered another with a scoop of ice cream on top to Lora.

She shook her head. "Let's meet with Sam first."

Addie took another cup from the carrier and poked a straw through the top. "I'll get the food set up." She glanced at me and smiled. "We have a ritual before a competition. We have the same food and drinks and wear the same outfits every time."

"Lots of people are like that," I said. With a nod to the offices behind me, I gestured to Lora and Nessa. "Ten minutes of your time."

The friends moved away from the island. Catherine grunted in loud dissatisfaction. "Lora, someone is after you, maybe wants to kill you. I don't think meditation is going to help with that."

Lora clutched a fist to her stomach.

Nessa spun to face her mom. "That is not helpful. Maybe you should just go home. I know you're worried, but with Walt here and Sam here, we've got it."

Catherine's mouth gaped open. She snatched up her purse off a barstool. "Don't say I didn't warn you."

Nessa held up her hand but said nothing more. She steered Lora and me into Nessa's office. I closed the office door and turned to face the friends.

"Do you want to hear this or has the day already been too much? What I have to say can wait."

Lora slumped into a chair. "That whole scene out there isn't anything new. Nessa and I are getting used to it."

I nodded. "Okay, then. I showed the letter to a friend I have on the force. He's going to look into it. Toby is trying to trace the IP address, but the person who sent it used a VPN—a virtual private network. I'm assuming you're familiar with how VPNs cloak IP addresses, so we might not get anywhere with that. Toby is also comparing all the other threats and where they were sent from to see if we can find a link or a thread or whatever."

They nodded in understanding.

I continued, "Some of the emails are signed by Caleb. Some are not. I find this odd. Some of the gifts sent, like the dead flowers, were bought at the grocery store in town. Walt tracked down the person who sold the flowers, and they described Caleb. Those were likely delivered by the person who bought the flowers and left them on your doorstep. The other stuff that was sent through the postal service does not appear to have originated at our post office. But a few were mailed in Vancouver. We're trying to link that to Caleb."

He doesn't have a car," Lora said. "How would he get those to a Vancouver post office?"

"Uber, Lyft, a friend. There are ways." I pushed forward with the really bad news. "Toby also found spyware on both of your computers, but not your phones. We're trying to track that as well. There doesn't seem to be an email with it attached. You know that sometimes people attach spyware to pictures or the like. We didn't see anything of that nature."

They gasped in unison.

"Spyware?" Lora said.

"Keylogging spyware to be specific. Toby thinks maybe to catch your keystrokes when gaming."

Lora gave a bitter laugh. "Joke's on them. I don't use my gaming computer for anything other than gaming. It's even on a different modem and home network. We use a VPN for that because of all the online issues with cyberbullying."

"Why would Caleb want to know your gaming keystrokes? Is he a competitor?"

Lora shook her head. "No, he's sometimes on my team. I share strategies with him. If Caleb's my stalker, I can see him using spyware to peep inside the house but not for attacking or hacking my game."

I sat on the edge of Nessa's desk and held up one hand. "This is weird. And I can see why you are hesitant to go after Caleb. On one hand, his emails are off. He does appear to have a crush on you, and some of his wording can appear as if he's threatening you. He says things like you're gonna get it. And watch your back."

Nessa said, "That's just Caleb and gaming talk. He's quirky. We've met him in person, and he's not scary at all."

I held up the other hand. "Yet, clearly, someone has targeted you and is trying to get you through gaming. Like yesterday's letter, their actions are untagged. Do you know if Caleb has any medical conditions? Maybe he's bipolar or something of that nature?" I tried to ask the question as gently as I could.

Lora shook her head. "I don't know. He's an introvert,

almost a hermit. He has a dry sense of humor that doesn't seem to go with his first impression. He can be quite funny."

Nessa nodded in agreement.

I was going to have to pay Caleb a visit sooner rather than later. "Toby made a clone of your computer, Lora. Your laptop. He has it up and running. Because we didn't sweep your gaming computer, which we need to do soon just to be sure. Can you leave your laptop up during the game so Toby can watch? We want to see if you get activity while you're online. And here is where I'm going to agree with Walt. We think, and so do the police, that this is a prime time for you to get another threat."

Lora and Nessa glanced nervously at each other.

I continued, "Unlike Walt, we're doing what we can to protect you online. We've got measures in place to track and record, should something happen."

Lora snapped her fingers and pointed to me. "I was just thinking the same thing. Ugh, he's infuriating."

I smiled but kept my mouth shut.

"We have about forty minutes until the game starts." Nessa pointed at her watch.

From her back pocket, Lora pulled out a ball cap. She slid it on pulling her ponytail through the back. "I think I'll get online and start making the rounds. Talk to some fans. Trash talk with some of the other gamers. This is my favorite part. Plus, I need to make sure Luke and Lance are online and ready to go."

"Lora's twin brothers often join our crew and compete. It's fun, and it's what people like about us," Nessa explained.

Lora chuckled as she stood. "It's particularly what the sponsors like about us. A family that plays together, stays together." She opened the office door and walked halfway across the foyer to her office before calling out, "Hey, Addie, I'm sorry to bother you. Could you bring me my tea?"

"Sure thing, Lora," Addie came into view and handed off a large cup. "The food is almost ready. I'll put the mochi out five minutes before the game starts so it doesn't melt." I put your other teas in the fridge for now."

"Can you just bring me a plate? Mix up the flavors, please."

Addie nodded and disappeared from view.

"Mochi?" I said.

Lora swirled the scoop of ice cream in her boba tea with a straw, then pulled the straw out, licking the ice cream off while she took a seat at her gaming station. "The first really big win I had, I was drinking boba tea and eating mochi. Comfort food for me. I don't need utensils and don't have to take my hands off the keyboard for long. Pizza is also on the menu." She slid on a headset and jiggled the mouse to activate her keyboard. Within seconds, she was online and chatting.

"How many of those will she go through?" I asked Nessa, pointing to the tea and thinking of the two carriers Addie had come in with.

"She has the blended one first. Then will move to milk teas. She will guzzle as many as we give her, but the acid is so hard on her stomach, we've limited her to four. Our goal is to wean her down to two." Nessa gestured to the door with her head. "Let's go out there and let her get into the zone."

We stepped out of the office. I glanced behind me, Lora's screen was up with a chat on one side and the game Shadowland Walker on the other.

"You don't miss playing?" I asked Nessa.

She shook her head. "I love it on occasion. I couldn't do

what Lora does. Games really amp me up, and I have a hard time sleeping afterward. Lora just rolls with it."

"So gaming didn't give her the ulcer?"

"Nope. That came more recently, when we started to get all these major opportunities. We pay all the people who will be on Lora's team tonight. Whether we win or not. Obviously, they get more if we win. But shifting from fun to business and adding in the threats... That's when she started to stress. Lora's paying for her brothers' college. We offer a scholarship every year for three others too. Keeping that funded is high priority for her. One more thing that adds stress."

"I see."

The doorbell chimed, and moments later, Addie came back into the kitchen carrying four boxes of pizza. She fanned them out on the counter, then glanced at her watch. "Mochi time." She hurried off to the pantry where the freezer was kept.

"Let me get my laptop. I'm going to join the chat." Nessa went to her office and came out seconds later with her laptop. She sat next to me at the island.

"Wait," I said. "Why didn't you mention you had a laptop? We haven't swept that."

Nessa grimaced. "I forget about it. I only use it on game nights. I get so sick of the computer, I rarely get on it after hours."

"Okay, we'll do it first thing tomorrow." I was so frustrated with myself. Not asking about other devices was a rookie mistake. Of course they had more than one computer. And they probably had tablets too.

Addie came back and turned the mochi box on its side dumping the trays of the little balls of ice cream on the counter. She ripped open the cellophane and tossed a few on a plate. She stuffed the remainder back in the box and returned to the pantry.

"Nessa," Lora said quietly from behind us.

We turned to where she stood outside her office, and I sprung to my feet. Lora was clutching her stomach and looked pale.

"What's the matter?" I rushed to her.

"I don't feel good. My stomach is killing me." She wobbled where she stood, and I caught her, leaning her against the wall.

Nessa rushed to her friend. "Did you take your meds? Want me to get them?"

Lora nodded. "It's not helping." She coughed, then licked her lips. Specks of blood dotted her lips like clotted lip gloss.

Nessa gasped.

I wrapped an arm around Lora's waist. "I'm taking you to the doctor. I think your ulcer is bleeding."

Lora leaned against me and doubled over. "Okay." To Nessa, she said. "Tell them I'm sorry I can't compete. That we have to cancel."

"Okay," Nessa said. "Okay."

"Unless you do it," Lora looked her friend in the eye. "It would be a fun twist. And I can use my phone to chime in on the chat. But only if you want."

Nessa looked into the office with the game pulled up on the screen. "The sponsors might like the sudden switch."

"And the fans love you. You know when you pop on, they get all excited." Lora let out a slow breath.

"Okay, I'll do it. It'll be fun."

Addie had come into the room and was holding a plate of mochi. "Is everything okay?"

Nessa took the plate. "We think Lora's ulcer is acting up. She's going to go to the doctor. I'm going to do the competition tonight." She showed the plate to me. "I used to hate these things. It's the dough around the ice cream. Grossed me out."

"But they've grown on you," Lora said with a clipped laugh. "Another one of my bad influences."

Nessa smiled. "Yes, but don't tell anyone. People like it when we spat about these things. Your love for them and my hate for them."

"One day, we'll have to come clean." Lora winced.

"Not today though," Nessa said and hugged her friend from the side. "Now, go get seen and hurry back."

CHAPTER FOUR

"I don't know why he's making me go to a hospital." Lora was slumped in the passenger seat of LC, her head against the window.

We'd made a call to her doctor to tell him what was going on, and he'd told us to go directly to the hospital. That's what we were doing.

I pressed the earpiece into place and waited for Toby to connect. At the house, we were using Lora's computer camera as our communication connection point, but now that Lora and I have left, Toby and I needed a new way to communicate.

"Your doc said he's being overly cautious. He said there's not anything to panic about, but he'd rather err on the side of caution."

"It's because he and my dad are friends," she mumbled.

"That probably plays a part. My dad runs the paper in town. Everyone knows him. My mom is the mayor. I can't go anywhere or do anything without them knowing about it." I turned right into the parking lot of the hospital and headed toward the emergency room. Lora's doctor said he'd meet us there.

"It must suck to be the mayor's kid." Lora wrapped her arms around her stomach and winced.

"Some days. How are you feeling? Better, worse?"

"Same."

"Sam, can you hear me?" Toby's voice crackled in my ear.

"Yeah, Toby, I hear ya."

"How's the game going?" Lora brought her cellphone screen to life. "Nessa's been quiet on the chat."

"Toby? How's the game?" I asked.

"Okay, so far. No activity. Normal smack talk and gaming. Team Darling is doing fine."

I relayed that back to Lora. "Okay, we're parking and going in. We might not have reception in the hospital because of the equipment. But I have my phone just in case."

"Roger," Toby replied.

I helped Lora out of the car and to the emergency room doors. Dr. Shavi, a tall dark-skinned man rushed to Lora as we came into view. He guided her into the wheelchair he'd had with him.

"Let's get you inside and start some tests." He nodded to me. "Thank you."

"Can she come with me, please?" Lora asked pointing to me.

Dr. Shavi gave me a quick look and then nodded.

"I'll push the chair," I said and stepped behind Lora, grabbing the wheelchair's handles. "Lead the way."

Inside the emergency room, he took us to a wing that was separated by real doors and not curtains. The room designated for Lora's care held a lot of intimidating equipment. Dr. Shavi took Lora's phone and purse and handed them both to me. "Wait out there." He pointed to the hallway outside the room.

I nodded to Lora and stepped out. Tucking her phone in the back pocket of my jeans, then slinging her purse over my shoulder crossbody style.

A nurse rushed in and began to set up a table. Moments later, she was writing down stats, then drawing blood. A few beats after that, the doctor and nurse stepped out of the room and drew a curtain in front of the door before closing it.

"She's changing," he said to me. To the nurse he said. "Set up a CAT scan. I'm going to call her dad. We might need to put her under to scope her if we can't get a good look. Find out what anesthesiologist is on call, please." The nurse nodded and scuttled off. Dr. Shavi stepped across the room and pressed a phone to his ear. The gadget in my ear emitted a static sound, like Toby was trying to reach me, but it wasn't coming through. I fidgeted with it a second, then took it out. I couldn't put up with that noise in my ear. I tucked the earpiece in the front pocket of my messenger bag.

The clanging of metal and scuffling of wheels came from down the hall, and I turned to see the paramedics wheeling in a man on a gurney, lots of wires and tubes connected to him. A second later, my mom came around the corner, a frantic look on her face. I glanced back at the man on the gurney.

"Dad?" My heart skipped a beat as the gurney swung out wide to enter the room next to Lora's, bringing Dad around to fully face me, his pale face pinched in pain.

"Mom?" I moved toward her.

She looked at me, confused. "Sam, how did you know? How did you—"

"I came with a client who was having stomach pains. What's going on?"

Mom's eyes welled with tears. "I think Dad's having a heart attack."

I reeled in shock. A different nurse and doctor rushed into Dad's room. People inside moved at lightning speed. Dad was lifted off the gurney to a table with such efficiency I would have been impressed, had I not been terrified.

I wrapped my arms around my mom as a different nurse put one hand up as a way to tell Mom to wait outside with me.

"I need to call Rachel," I said. My older sister lived on the East Coast with my six-year-old niece, Cora. Rachel was in the Navy.

Mom shook her head. "Not yet. Let's get all the facts first." Mom was right. Rachel was a nurse and would have a million questions.

Dr. Shavi and his nurse returned to Lora's room, and Mom and I remained outside in a holding pattern. Against my hip, a phone vibrated. And then again and again. But all I could do was watch what was unfolding in my dad's room and wonder what was happening in Lora's.

What felt like forever passed before Dr. Shavi came out of Lora's room.

"She's going to be okay. We're giving her some medicine now and making her comfortable." He looked into the other room where Dad was and raised a brow.

"My father," I said. My arm was still wrapped around my mom. I had my dad's height but my mom's reddish-blonde hair and light eyes. Anyone could see we were related.

Dr. Shavi put a hand on my mom's shoulder. "Everything looks under control in there, and Dr. Alexander is amazing. Why don't I take you both to the waiting room. They'll come there first to find you when they have an update." He nudged us down the hall and into a small room off to the side. He eased Mom into a chair.

"We were having dinner, and he started rubbing his shoulder. Saying it ached. I... I teased him about being old and maybe having a heart attack. How terrible is that?" Mom looked at me with wide, shocked eyes.

"Mom, it's not terrible. You couldn't have known."

"Only I think I did. He was clenching his jaw, and my gut just said something wasn't right. I asked if he was okay, and when he paused, I decided to call nine-one-one."

"You did everything right," Dr. Shavi said. "And because your response was so quick, we have more treatment options." He patted Mom's shoulder. "You and your daughter have good instincts. She's helped my patient get quick treatment as well. I'm going to step out and check on Lora."

"Thank you, Doctor."

He patted my shoulder too, then left.

I sat next to Mom, holding her hand. We waited in silence. The world around me had narrowed. My focus and thoughts only for my family and our crisis at hand.

Twenty minutes later, a doctor entered the room. He extended his hand to mom.

"I'm Dr. Alexander." They shook.

"Elizabeth True. This is my daughter Samantha. How's Russ?"

Dr. Alexander smiled. "He's doing well. He did have a mild heart attack, but we were able to manage it well. We're going to keep him overnight for observation. They're getting a room for him now. But you both can go see him if you want."

Mom and I sprang to our feet.

"Thank you, Dr. Alexander. Thank you so much," Mom said.

"Well, the hard work starts now. Diet changes, exercise. But we can go over all that later." Dr. Alexander had a kind smile.

I followed Mom into Dad's room and nearly burst into tears. He looked so frail and weak on the bed, with all the wires and tubes.

"Sammy, did I see you as I was coming in?" Dad asked in a raspy voice.

Always a reporter, my dad. Even as he's entering a hospital while having a heart attack, he noticed his surroundings.

"Yeah, I brought a client in who wasn't feeling well. Looks like both of you are having a good outcome to an unlucky night." I rushed to my dad and dropped a kiss on his forehead. "You scared me."

The phone on my hip vibrated again.

"Me too," Mom said and took his hand.

"Me three," he said and closed his eyes. "I guess I have to give up things like cheese and real food."

Mom chuckled. "I think moderation is key here. And maybe reduce your stress."

"Says the woman running a town." He opened his eyes. "For a second when I saw you, Sam, I thought you were hurt. Scared me."

Stress. I'd stressed him out.

"Me, hurt? Nah."

"A cat only has nine lives," Dad said with a knowing look. He was referring to cases I'd had. Ones where I'd been shot at and blown up and yeah ... had my share of hospital visits.

"Says the man with all the tubes and wires." He'd taught me everything I knew about misdirection. "I'm going to step out and call Rachel."

Mom nodded her approval. I gave Dad another kiss before exiting.

I pulled out my cell phone and saw thirty-two text messages and twelve missed calls. I glanced into Lora's room. The curtain had been pulled back, and a young guy stood in there, shaking his finger at Lora. He didn't look to be hospital staff.

I stuffed my phone in my back pocket, then pushed open her door. Cutting off the guy midsentence. "Is everything okay in here?"

"This is Caleb," Lora said.

It took a few seconds for my brain to catch up. "*Caleb* Caleb?" As in the stalker?

She nodded.

He swung his attention to me. "I was telling Lora that she's next. First Nessa and then her. She has to be aware of The Shadow Man. He is out to get us all. I'm warning you." His face was flushed. Spittle flew out of his mouth as he spoke. Caleb was clearly agitated.

I reached for my messenger bag and the stun gun inside. "Okay," I said. "Consider her warned. But you're also scaring her. And she's in the hospital, so she can't afford to be scared right now."

"She can't afford to not be scared right now." He spun back to face Lora. "You're next. You need to do a better job of being careful."

I agreed with that because how did he know Lora was at the hospital, and more importantly, how did he get in her room?

"Caleb," I said. "I'm Samantha. I'm friends with Lora, and I'm here to help her. I'm here to help keep her safe. Why don't you step outside with me, and we can talk about this?" My brain was frazzled from the events of the last hour, and I was running on fumes and instinct. Leo would probably yell at me for offering to leave with the guy who was under suspicion as Lora's stalker. I mean, he did just threaten her.

He shook his head. "I'm not going anywhere with you. And neither should Lora." To her he said, "Trust no one."

"Caleb," I said.

"No!" he shouted. "No." And he rushed from the room and down the hall.

"Are you okay?" I asked Lora.

She nodded. "Just shaken up. Can I get my phone? I want to see how the game is going."

Phone. My brain flashed the image of my phone's screen with all the missed calls and messages. Something had happened. And if our luck for the night was any indicator, whatever had happened was probably not good. Not good at all. I held up one finger and pulled out my phone.

Toby had called twelve more times. I hit callback.

He answered on half a ring. "Jeez, Sam, where've you been?" His voice wobbled in fear.

"What's happened?"

"Nessa collapsed. Addie called the paramedics. From

what I could see through the camera, she wasn't very responsive."

"Wasn't very? What does that mean?" Dread coiled in my stomach like a large heavy mass.

"I think Nessa is dead."

CHAPTER FIVE

SHORTLY AFTER NESSA ARRIVED AT THE HOSPITAL, SHE was pronounced dead on arrival. Her mother arrived shortly after, and upon hearing the news, promptly fell apart. But I expected nothing less. Not from Lora either. When she found out Nessa had died, she'd come undone and had to be sedated. Telling her had been the worst thing I'd done at this job. Ever.

The next morning, I stood in the bowels of the local hospital, desperate for answers.

Leo held a manila folder in his hand and pressed his lips together, thinning them.

"What does the ME say?" I held out my hand for the report pressed inside the file folder.

"Its preliminary, of course, but he's leaning toward accidental overdose. Vanessa had a heart condition and was on a daily dose of Warfarin."

"And the ME thinks she took too much of that?" The plausibility sounded skeptical to me. "Was this heart condition new?"

Leo shook his head. "She had it since she was a child."

I crossed my arms. Instinctively, the tingle in my gut told me something wasn't right, I just couldn't put my finger on what precisely. And truthfully, maybe it was the trauma of losing Nessa that was upsetting my gut. Maybe nothing was wrong except that a young woman in her prime was now dead. A woman I'd seen alive just hours ago.

"How much does a person have to take to have an accidental overdose? One pill?"

He shook his head. "I'm guessing a few more than that."

"I was with Nessa yesterday. She wasn't confused or haggard from running around. She was calm and steady. I'm finding this hard to believe." I shook my head to make my point.

Leo slid an arm around my shoulders and pulled me against him. "Is the alternative any better?"

I rested my head on his shoulder. "I can't imagine Nessa would harm herself."

"And that is why it's an accidental overdose." He kissed my forehead. "I feel like I haven't seen you in days."

I snuggled into him. "That case you were working on was sucking up a lot of time. I hope it's wrapping up."

"Auto insurance fraud. DB had us do a sting operation, and lucky for him, it all wrapped up tight."

DB, the local police chief, had gone to high school with Leo and me. At one point, we'd been forced to be chemistry partners, and he'd cheated off me ... a girl with dyslexia. He's not so bright.

"So maybe we can have dinner one night soon?" I asked, wrapping my arms around his waist. If anyone had told me Leo Stillman and I would be dating, I would have laughed in their face. We'd never been close. And then one day, my husband turned up dead, also legally not my husband, and some scary guys he'd done business with had come looking for me to fill in the blanks.

Leo had been more than reliable during a time when I had no idea what was fact and what was fiction. But also, he'd been a literal lifesaver.

Now here we were dating. Weird, I know. And to complicate matters, my dead husband showed up alive a few weeks back bringing with him the news that one of the bad guys I'd put away had put a hit on me.

But that wasn't my problem today. Lora and Nessa were my focus and concern. My client was dead.

"We could go grab something in the hospital cafeteria right now if you want."

"I need to talk to Lora. How about later tonight?" I pressed my nose to his neck and inhaled. There was so much about Leo that was comforting, but his outdoorsy smell—fir trees and bergamot—helped me find my center.

"That might work."

"At my place, then?"

He stroked a hand down my hair. "We can try, babe. We can try." The skepticism in his voice told me he wasn't counting on it. Truthfully, neither was I, but at least we were trying.

I pushed away and looked up at him. "I want to talk with Lora before I leave. I have a meeting with Toby, and then I want to go by my dad's to see how he's doing. He was released this morning. If all goes well, I should be home by—"

He pressed a finger to my lips. "Shh, don't say it out loud. I think the universe takes it as a challenge. Let's just leave it at us trying." He winked.

I nipped at the finger pressed to my lips. "Deal." I

pushed away and started down the hallway. I stopped and turned. "If the ME is ruling Nessa's death an accidental overdose, then I'm assuming, to the police, it's open and shut. No investigation."

"That's a correct assumption. You're gonna have to give me something more substantial if you think something is off here. And because *you're* the PI for this girl, it's unlikely if you do find anything worthy, that DB will assign me the case. So you know, whatever you find is gonna have to be solid."

"Noted," I said, then blew him a kiss. I made my way up a few floors to Lora's room. Her parents were sitting next to her bed as I entered.

I gave a small wave. "How ya holding up?"

She shook her head, and tears flowed down her face. "I just can't believe it. How could this happen?" Her eyes pleaded with me to have an answer. I needed to tread cautiously, as Lora's parents didn't know I was a PI, and Lora had asked me not to tell them. She didn't want them to worry needlessly.

I weighed what to say; what was too little information? What was too much?

But Lora's dad beat me to it.

The tall man had just enough gut to hang over his belt. He wore Birkenstocks with socks, and Lora told me he was a homeopathic doc who specialized in acupuncture.

He took Lora's hand in his. "Honey, I spoke to Catherine. She said Nessa accidentally took too much of her heart medicine. That's what caused the overdose."

Lora's mom, an older version of Lora, medium height with graying dark hair and lots of laugh lines stood and wrapped an arm around her daughter, comforting her.

"That's impossible." Lora shook her head wildly. "Nessa

kept her paper journal with a checklist of when she filled her pill organizer, when she took her meds. She had alerts set on her phone. She was diligent about checks and balances because she knew her meds were serious business. She would joke about them. Called them rat poison. Said she didn't want to be exterminated." Lora choked back a sob and swiped the back of her hands across her eyes. "It's not possible."

I swallowed hard, fighting back the lump in my throat. Nessa had been so young. So full of life. Maybe I wanted to imagine the worst because that made more sense than an accident. A miscount.

Lora's mother cooed and brushed her child's hair. Lora shook her off. Dejected, her mother took a seat next to Lora's father.

"Sam," Lora began, her gaze boring into mine. "You have to..." She looked between her parents.

I knew where she was going. She wanted me to look into this. "You're going to stay with your folks, right?"

Lora nodded. "I can't go home just yet."

"How about I go home and grab some of your things? I can bring them to your parents' house."

Lora caught on quick. Her eyes widened slightly. "Yes, go to the house. Let me make you a list of what I need." On her bedside table was a notebook. She scratched out a list, ripped off the paper, then handed it to me. On it she'd written where Nessa kept her pillbox and instructions to check that and Nessa's journal which should be in her room or office.

I nodded. "Can I use the same code to get in?"

"Two, two, zero, two, six," they said in unison.

"Wait, everyone has the same code?"

Lora nodded.

That wasn't good. But I'd tackle that when Lora was ready. I tucked the paper in my pants pocket. "I'll see you soon."

I stepped out of her room and saw Dr. Shavi talking with a nurse. I waited for the nurse to leave before I approached the doctor.

He nodded once in greeting. "Lora says she's going home with her parents."

"Yes, I'm off to get her some things from the house," I said. "Can you answer a question for me?"

He raised a brow, a signal for me to continue.

"Lora has a stomach ulcer. What would ingesting Warfarin do to that ulcer?"

He lowered the clipboard he'd been holding. "Depends on how much, it could cause a person to bleed out if not caught in time."

"You did a blood test on Lora yesterday, correct?"

"Well, I can't really say what I did and didn't do, but I believe you saw something like that through the window." He waited patiently for me to get to the point.

"Can you test Lora'a blood for Warfarin?" Instantly, his expression went hard.

"Now, I don't know what you're implying, and what's happened to Vanessa Taylor was tragic, but I can't see how that would affect Lora. Particularly if Vanessa ingested all that extra medicine accidentally."

I knew what he meant. That Nessa hadn't been monitoring her daily dose and made a mistake, taking in more than prescribed.

But I had a different worry. "If Nessa might have accidentally ingested too much Warfarin, maybe Lora did as well. Maybe Nessa liked to put the meds in her food to mask the taste. I don't know. But peace of mind would sure be great. Because I can't imagine that taking one extra pill would have caused Nessa to die? Am I wrong?"

He shook his head.

"And what if this wasn't Nessa's fault at all. What if the food they ate was contaminated? What if any minute now, there's going to be a recall because rat poison fell into a vat at some manufacturers' site? Crazy, but not impossible, right?"

He sighed. "Not impossible. I suppose I could check." He was dragging his heels.

"I would really appreciate it if you would. I'll share all this with Lora after I get her stuff, and you can tell her what you've found when you get the results."

"She's very fragile," he said. His persistent hesitancy made me take the next step.

"Yes, but she might also be in danger." I pulled out my PI badge. "Lora and Nessa had a stalker, and I was hired two days ago to find that person. Lora's parents don't know any of this yet. And I wouldn't be telling you if I wasn't concerned for her safety. I believe you knowing who I am gives my request some validity."

"A stalker?" He pressed a finger to his temple. "Of course, I'll check her blood for Warfarin and other toxins as well. Thanks for the heads-up."

We separated after that. The lab required days before they could get the tox screening done. In the meantime, all I had were my hunches.

Could Lora and Vanessa have been poisoned? And if so, why was I the only one who thought this might be a possibility?

CHAPTER SIX

An hour later, I made it to Lora's house, keyed in the security code, and entered. Still stunned that everyone was using the same keycode.

The house was spotless.

I expected a mess.

Who had the time to come clean up after all that had happened?

I did a quick walk through of Lora's office, trying to get a feel for what had happened last night. Nothing looked out of place.

From there, I moved through Nessa's office, the living room, and into the kitchen. Nothing appeared out of place. The marble counters were so clean they shined. The dishwasher was running.

A muted bang came from either the garage or beyond it.

I slipped my hand into my messenger bag, touching the familiar and comforting shape of my stun gun. I made my way through the kitchen, and coasted silently into the butler's pantry, heading toward the garage door. I stopped by the freezer and opened it. Just a few days ago, it had been stocked with mochi, pizza rolls, and Beecher's mac and cheese. All the mochi was gone, as were the pizza rolls. The freezer was empty except for two lonely mac-and-cheese boxes.

I eased the door closed and moved to enter the garage. A scuffle came from the other side. I pulled out my stun gun. Then I eased open the door.

Addie was lifting a trash bag, preparing to swing it onto the bed of a pickup truck.

"What are you doing?" I asked.

She jumped, screamed, and dropped the bag. It clanged when it hit the ground. She spun to face me, her hand to her chest. She was wearing yellow plastic dishwashing gloves, and they stood out against her black tunic and black leggings.

"You scared me to death," she said, then covered her mouth in horror. "I don't mean *death* death. Oh God, this is awful." Tears sprung to her eyes.

I pointed to the truck. "What's all this?"

Addie slumped against the tailgate of the truck. "Walt asked me to clean up. He wants the place sterilized for Catherine. Said she was coming over later, and the place needed to be clean and devoid of anything that was going to trigger Catherine about what happened."

"So you single-handedly cleaned this place?"

Addie shook her head. "I called in our cleaning people. They came on short notice and helped me get it all together. I don't know what he means by devoid of reminders because Nessa lived here. I don't know what to do with her stuff." She burst into tears. "This is just awful. How could this have happened?"

I put my stun gun away. "Whose truck is this?"

"Walt's. He said Catherine is a bit unhinged and looking for answers. I mean, I get that. Nessa was her only child, and this whole situation"—her breath hitched—"makes zero sense. He said when he brings her here to get an outfit for Nessa's..." She swallowed hard.

I waved her off. She didn't have to say the word funeral. And I didn't want her to repeat what she just said. Addie seemed to be stuck on a loop. "Where is Walt?"

"Around here somewhere." She wiped her cheeks.

"Okay, thanks." I went back into the house to look for Walt and the pillbox. My first stop was Nessa's office. I rummaged quickly through the drawers with my ears peeled for movement in the house.

No journal. No pillbox. Nothing out of the ordinary. A calendar marked with future events and scheduled meetings. I lifted the calendar and found a Post-it with a wish list. In Nessa's neat print was a list of what she wanted to do for the company. Getting a sponsorship was number one, and a smiley face was next to it. Nessa had big ideas for her and Lora's company. But not pie-in-the-sky ideas.

I set the calendar back over the note. One day, maybe Lora would be willing to pursue Nessa's dreams.

I climbed the stairs to the bedrooms. Nessa's was the front room, and the door was open. I entered slowly, expecting to find Walt, except the room was empty. Nessa's room was as tidy as her office. Had Addie cleaned it? Or was this who Nessa was? I leaned toward the latter. Nessa had a sharp mind and a clear vision for her company, and that took a disciplined person. And if it was as Lora said, that Nessa kept a journal and used a pillbox, then my beliefs were probably smack on.

Nessa had her own bathroom, and I started with the

medicine cabinet. Sure enough, there was Nessa's weekly pillbox. The containers for Monday through Thursday were empty. The pills for the rest of the week were intact with the container lid closed. Next to the pillbox was the prescription bottle. I bent to look it over. The fill date was thirty days ago, and the prescription had been filled for forty-five days. She was due to get another refill in the next week. I took pictures with my cell phone, making sure not to touch anything. I then went through the drawers and under the sink, looking for the journal. But I found nothing remarkable. No rat poison or any other prescriptions. Just facial masks, tampons, makeup, hair products, and nail polish.

In Nessa's room, I found the journal on her bedside table. Using a pen from my messenger bag, I flipped the journal open and found the page where she had logged everything. Nessa was very artsy, and her journal pages were decorated beautifully. She had colored in the block and logged the time she'd taken her meds on Thursday: 8:23 a.m. I took photos of the pages, leaving the journal behind for her mother.

I slid open the drawer of her bedside table and picked through the paperback books she'd stowed there.

"Hey!" a man's voice boomed behind me. "What are you doing?"

I jumped and slammed the drawer before spinning to face Walt.

"Sorry, I was..." I had nothing, so I switched gears. "I'm sorry about Nessa. I could have helped with the cleanup." And maybe poked around a bit more while doing so.

He gestured for me to leave the room. "I'm bringing her mother here in a few hours, and I want that to be the least traumatic experience possible."

"I get it. I—"

"Which means Lora can't be here either. In fact, I'm not sure how Catherine is going to handle seeing Lora at all. She needs to stay away."

"Wait. What? Why? This is Lora's house. You can't keep her out of it." I stood in the hallway, blocking the stairs. I crossed my arms.

Walt ran a hand through his close-cropped buzz cut. He looked tired. Likely, he was the one person keeping Catherine together, if I had to guess.

"Right now, Catherine is looking for someone to blame. She's lost her only child. And she can't make sense of it. Particularly because there's the possibility that Nessa, maybe..." He cleared his throat. "Maybe this was intentional."

He said the last part in a hushed voice. As if saying the words were too awful. This was not the behavior of a seasoned PI, in my opinion. But then he had history with the family, so I guess I understood his professionalism slipping some.

"You think this was intentional?" I had hoped that I wasn't the only one who thought things weren't right.

He shook his head. "Whatever I think doesn't matter. I'm going with what the ME is saying."

It took a moment for me to process what he meant. I leapt to murder. He was leaping elsewhere.

"Is there anything to explain that possibility? Have you found a note?" Truthfully, I couldn't believe Nessa had died by suicide either. Because to do so meant Nessa had been hurting and maybe we'd missed the signs. Though that felt impossible, the truth was, I'd only known Nessa a few days, and I'd come to believe that anything was possible. I mean, my dead husband was actually alive, and I'd seen the remains of his car after his fiery crash.

Walt shook his head. "None of it makes sense, and because of that, the possibility this might have been suicide will always haunt Catherine. Sadly."

"This stalker Lora told me about, Caleb, right?"

Walt nodded.

"He came to the hospital last night. Was very agitated. Are any of his threats geared toward Nessa? Could there be something more sinister here?"

Walt stuck his hands in the pockets of his dress pants. "That was my first thought. But I'd run through every scenario, and I can't find a thread. Lora was the stalker's focus. But you shouldn't concern yourself with any of that. You were hired to help Lora, right? With her getting her life on track. I'm guessing she's going to need that more than ever."

"I'm here to pick up some of her things. She's going to be staying with her folks for a while, so you won't have to worry about Catherine running into her when you bring her here."

He nodded once.

I turned toward Lora's room but stopped halfway and faced him, finding it hard to believe he wasn't suspicious about Nessa's death. "I know you've ruled out Caleb, at least in Nessa's death, but at the hospital he said that Nessa's death wasn't an accident. That Lora was next. You shouldn't—"

"Don't tell me what I should and shouldn't do. If that threat scared her, then maybe she'll do something now, maybe she'll file the restraining order. She should stay off social media, too. As you know as a life coach, there are fans, and there are haters, and they've come out in droves because of Nessa's death."

Walt wasn't giving me much. And he seemed unbothered by Caleb showing up at the hospital moments after Nessa died and all the threats he was reporting against Lora. I wanted more from Walt, but clearly, he kept his cards close.

I went into Lora's room, feeling his eyes on my back. From under her bed, I withdrew her suitcase and began putting the items she requested in the case. When Walt finally moved away, going downstairs as quietly as he'd come up them, I texted Toby and told him to start scouring the net to look for possible threads.

Everything seemed off here, and I was determined to figure out what the actual hell was going on.

CHAPTER SEVEN

THAT AFTERNOON, THE SUN CAME OUT AND SHONE brightly, though the day didn't feel bright at all.

The negative social media posts regarding Lora and Nessa were disturbing.

I scrolled through the summary of the posts and comments Toby had sent me as I waited for Lora at a picnic table in the park near her house. Dressed in jeans and a hoodie, I was thankful for the vitamin D but enjoying the much cooler weather. Toby had sorted the posts by thread theme. Some people envied Lora for her fame. Some people hated that young girls were doing so well and kept their post about how women should stay in their lane. Whatever that means. Some posts were from other gamers who Lora or Nessa had bested, and these gamers weren't very good sports. A few accused Lora of stifling Nessa, hogging the fame for herself and alluding to Nessa being unhappy with no alternative but to end everything. Not one thread hinted at murder. Not one thread was what you'd expect from a stalker who just ended his victim's life because they had no choice.

Yeah, there were threads from Caleb. Many saying Lora was in trouble. And they could be interpreted like a threat. But to me, they seemed more like a warning. Caleb's threads were not organized in structure. They rambled almost frantically. And they were alarming by that measure alone.

Lora joined me a few minutes later. Her hair was in a sloppy ponytail, and her face was devoid of makeup. She was wearing loose pants and a baggy sweatshirt. Dark circles were under her eyes.

"Not sleeping, huh?" I asked.

She shook her head. "Did you find Nessa's pill organizer and journal? I was right, wasn't I? She didn't do this accidentally."

"Before we go into all that, have you heard from your doctor? Remember, I asked him to test for toxins on the blood he drew." I'd told Lora to expect the results.

She pulled a phone out from her pocket and tapped the screen. She showed me an email. "This came this morning. I'm not sure what it means."

I scanned the email from Dr. Shavi. There was no meat to the email, just some lab numbers. I studied the screen, taking the time to let my mind work out the numbers and connect the dots. Then I handed Lora back her phone.

"You don't believe that Nessa could have accidentally taken too many Warfarin pills, right?"

Lora nodded.

"Her mother fears Nessa might have taken them on purpose."

Lora gasped and covered her mouth. She began to shake her head, her eyes wet with unshed tears.

"But that email"—I pointed to her phone—"says you had Warfarin in your system as well. Not enough to do real harm but enough to irritate your ulcer."

Lora sat motionless, hands pressed over her mouth. The furrow of her brow told me she was processing what I'd just told her.

She dropped her hands. "You think Nessa was murdered? And someone tried to off me too?"

I cleared my throat. "I think, of the three options, murder is the most likely of scenarios. I didn't see anything in Nessa's office or room to indicate that she would harm herself. Though to be fair, Addie had the house cleaned and scoured by the time I'd arrived. So maybe she also threw things away." I shrugged. "I can't be sure. But I did find Nessa's journal, and she did keep meticulous records of when she filled her pillbox, when she took her pills, and even when she had her prescription filled. I saw that meticulousness throughout all her work. If Nessa was going to hurt herself, I can't help but think that would have shown up in her work and everything."

In a rush of words, Lora said, "Murdered. How did we get here? Could Caleb have done that? Were we wrong? He was so scary at the hospital a few days ago."

"I'm looking into Caleb. I do think it's odd how he knew to get to the hospital to see you and how he knew about Nessa before it was confirmed. But I'm not focused solely on him. Lora, the cops, Nessa's mom, and even Walt don't suspect murder. There's a chance I could be wrong." I didn't think I was, but there's always the chance.

"You aren't. It's the only option that makes sense, as weird as that sounds." She looked away, lost in thought. "If I could have stopped this... If only—"

"Stop right there," I interrupted. "*No one* saw this coming. You can't blame yourself." For the last forty-eight hours I'd beaten myself up wondering how I'd missed the signs of an attack. Wondering what it was that I couldn't see but was likely right in front of me. "You have two choices. You can cease everything and just cope with healing. Or you can keep me on, or even hire someone else, to get to the bottom of this. I should warn you that if you pick the second option then things could get very ugly before they get better." They always did. Righting a wrong was not easy or pretty. "Think about it."

"I don't have to," Lora said. "I can't let this go. Nessa deserves better. She deserves to be alive, and the person who took that from her needs to pay."

"Okay," I said, nodding. I took her hand. "If you want a different private investigator—"

"I want you. I trust you." She squeezed my hand. She glanced over my shoulder. "Look, there's Catherine. I've been calling her."

Lora sprang up from the picnic table. As did I.

"Lora, wait," I called, but Lora was jogging across the grass to the sidewalk where Catherine was walking. The normally perfectly coiffed woman looked disheveled. She wore her hair down, ratted in the back. Her trousers were wrinkled, her shirt partially tucked in as if she'd attempted to dress, but decided the effort was too much, and she'd given up.

"Catherine," Lora called. "Catherine, I'm so sorry." Lora's voice broke as she stumbled but caught herself. Within seconds, she was in front of Nessa's mom.

Catherine reared back, hands on her chest. She looked at Lora as if she'd witnessed Lora do something heinous.

"Get away from me," Catherine hissed. "Get away."

I caught up to Lora and put my hand on her elbow. "Let's let Mrs. Siegel be."

Lora shook me off and reached out for Catherine. "I'm so sorry. I don't know why anyone would do this to Nessa. I'm so sorry."

"Do this to Nessa? You did this to my daughter. She's dead because of you. You held her back, you kept everything she wanted for yourself. That's why my daughter is dead."

Lora shuffled back in horror and confusion. "What are you talking about? I didn't—"

"Mrs. Seigel, certainly you can't think Lora had anything to do with this tragedy." I tried to tuck Lora behind me.

"I didn't murder my best friend," Lora screamed. "How could you think that?"

Catherine gasped. "Murdered? Nessa wasn't murdered. She was distraught. Empty. Sad. Because of you."

I tried to defuse the situation. "Maybe you should consider that Nessa might have been intentionally harmed. Lora had—"

"Nessa *was* harmed, by the life she and this ... this ... so-called friend of hers lived. How dare you both try to say someone hated my daughter enough to end her life. How dare you try to turn this into something to tweet or post about. I am barely hanging on here. And ... and ... and what you're saying is incomprehensible. And what proof do you have? None. But I have proof. If my daughter was so happy, why did she hire a life coach?" Catherine looked right at me. "Explain that to me. Explain what she wanted to improve in her life."

I shook my head, having no answer. How could I tell her I wasn't a life coach but a PI because Nessa hadn't trusted her mother's choice in PI's. That was the last thing Catherine needed to hear.

When I said nothing. Her lips curled.

"You both disgust me." She pushed past us, swinging her arms wildly as if blindly striking out.

Lora lunged after her, but I caught her, wrapping my arms around her.

"Leave her be," I said quietly in Lora's ear. "She's grieving and needs a target. That's you."

Lora's knees buckled. "But why? I'm grieving too."

"I know, but there's no explaining how people cope with loss. I didn't know Nessa's mom lived by your parents."

Lora nodded. "One street over. That's how we became so close. We had the same class in third grade. We rode the same bus and played in the same neighborhood. She's been my best friend since then."

I put my arm across her shoulder and steered her in the opposite direction. "Come on, let me get you home."

CHAPTER EIGHT

Forty minutes passed before I managed to get Lora to calm down and return her safely home to her mother's arms. The accusations Catherine made had shaken Lora to the core, restarting the grieving process.

I left Lora's and went immediately to my parents. Dad had been discharged the same time as Lora. I'd been banned from hovering over my dad for the first twenty-four hours; my parents had both told me to focus on the case, knowing I didn't do idle well. Focusing on the case was easy to do because what was happening with my father was scary and hard to face. A heart attack? He was so young.

I pulled into the driveway and sat for a few minutes letting LC idle. Call me naïve or immature or whatever, but I wasn't ready to picture a life without my mom or dad in it. And thinking of losing them made me think of Catherine and what she must be going through having lost her only child.

Sucking in a handful of deep calming breaths, I steadied my nerves and pasted a smile on my face, because the last thing Dad needed was one more family member freaked out. I'm sure my mother was hovering, and Rachel was texting all the time to check his stats. For her, being his nurse was easier than being his daughter. Knowing his stats made her feel proactive.

Inside, I found Dad on the couch, a blanket over his legs, the sports channel on TV. He was so pale, but not as bad as the day he'd been rolled into the hospital, so by those standards, he looked pretty good. He was texting on his phone.

"Hey," I said.

He immediately went to hide his phone, tucking it under the blanket, until he registered it was me and not my mom. He took his phone back out. "Don't tell your mother. I'm not supposed to be working."

"So don't work!" I held out my hand to take his phone.

He shook his head. "I'm just texting Stella about things to do with the newspaper. I'm not really working. Working would be writing articles. I'm managing the business."

"Managing still sounds like working. And what were the doctor's orders?" I sank into the couch by his feet, letting my body relax.

"The doctor's orders were to rest. Change my diet and decrease stress. All done. Check, check, check." He gave me a pointed look. "Don't forget I'm the parent; and you are the child."

"Yeah, but I'm the child who can't live without her parent."

Dad's face softened. "I know this seems scary, but it was a mild heart attack, caught really early, and there's no reason to think that it will happen again now that we know, and now that I can make some changes."

"Yeah, but Dad, changing your diet doesn't mean that it

won't happen again, and you can't guarantee that something else won't happen. It's just scary."

"Says the daughter who last year was in a house explosion and who was the target in a drive-by shooting."

I bit my lip, because how does one respond to that. I had seen far more danger in my last year than he'd seen ... ever.

"And knowing these things about me is probably causing you some stress. Like when I saw them wheel you into the hospital, that caused me stress, worry, and anxiety."

"Oh, Sam, I've worried about you from the minute you took your first step. That's what parents do. We worried when we gave you peanuts for the first time, and when you went on a date, or drove the first time alone. That's what parents do. If you were working in a school or a hospital like your sister, I would worry. And yeah, the fact that you have a job that puts you at risk maybe increases my stress a little bit but that's not on you. That's for me to manage."

I'd been wanting to grow my PI business beyond insurance investigations and into more lucrative opportunities. But lucrative meant more risk, and more risk meant more stress for my parents. I didn't want to be the reason my dad was sick.

I thought back to all the times he'd come to see me in the hospital, always a smile on his face. Yet probably behind that smile, he'd been masking fear. And I'd done that to him. I looked at Dad, shook my head, tears filling my eyes. "I love you, Daddy-o. I'm sorry for ever having added to any of your stress."

"Oh, honey. There's nothing to be sorry about." He scooted across the couch and wrapped his arms around me.

"Hey." I hugged him back. "I came here to see if I could

help take care of you, not the other way around. I didn't want to make you sad."

He chuckled and kissed my temple. "Seeing you always makes me happy. It always takes away from my stress." He lingered with the hug, and I buried my face in his shoulder like I'd done when I was a little kid. Finding comfort in the familiarity that was my dad. We broke apart a few seconds later.

"So tell me what the doctor said, besides change your diet, decrease your stress, etc."

Dad pointed to a pillbox on the coffee table. "He said to take those, and if I can get my diet under control, I might even be able to reduce some of those pills. So for now, that medication stays attached to my body, according to your mother. I take them three times a day."

I thought of Nessa's journal and her careful notes. On the table next to his pillbox was a small notebook: Dad's way of tracking his intake.

"How can I help with the newspaper?" I asked.

"I think Stella's got it under control. I have Dan helping her with uploads, and she's got emails out to the freelancers. I'll tell her to call you if she needs another set of hands." Dan was my dad's webmaster.

"Toby can help Dan if he needs it."

Dad squeezed my hand. "Speaking of Toby, he told me about your case. You think your stalker is at the root of this?"

"When did you talk to Toby?"

"While I was in the hospital, when I got home, today. He calls during his high time. He likes to chat."

Toby's high time was the part of the day he took off work to get stoned, eat all the food, and I thought watch movies and chill, but apparently, it was also the time he called my dad.

Dad continued, "So I looked into this kid, Caleb. I'm putting together a file for you. Other posts he's made. He's very chatty online and sometimes he's not very nice."

"Dad, the PI Walt already did that. I've seen the posts. You don't need—"

"I want to help you and Toby. I can't just be idle. Besides, context. You always have to consider context. Did you read his posts from start to finish?"

I shook my head, "What I saw were snippets."

"Then you aren't getting the whole picture."

"Okay fine, get me those threads. But then take some time to be idle."

"I'll lose my mind."

My mom hustled into the room carrying a tray. "Okay, Russell. I know you're gonna complain when you see what's on this tray, but you're going to eat every bite of this." She looked up, spotted me, and grinned. "Hello, Samantha. I didn't hear you come in."

"Hey, Mama. Can I help with anything?"

"Nope. Not unless you know how to get your father to comply." She smiled warmly and set the tray on my father's lap. He looked at the plate of food, and his lip curled. "Is that kale? You know I don't like kale." He pointed to a salad.

"It's mixed with a lot of other greens that will help you choke it down." Mom stood over Dad with her hands on her hips. She meant business.

"I am not going to live my life trying to choke something down. That's not living, but I get I need greens. Is there something else that we can use instead of kale, something to replace it, like a pill? I'll happily take a vitamin. I don't want to eat kale. It tastes nasty."

He picked some of the leaves off his plate and flicked them onto the tray.

I stood. "Well, I see things are going as expected here." I reached out and hugged my mother. "Leo and I have a date tonight, so no one should be stressed about that."

Dad continued to flick kale. "Leo is good. Safe."

"Love Leo. Love you and Leo together." My mom clapped her hands with happiness. "It's about time."

"So says everyone," I mumbled. "Text or call me if you need me and I'll pop in tomorrow or the next day and see how things are going. I'll call Rachel and see if she can relax a bit. I'm sure that she's texting you all the time. I could try to make her feel better about everything."

Dad let his head fall back against the couch. "Oh, that would be wonderful. Sometimes I'm right into a good nap, and she'll text, and if I don't respond right away, she'll call, worried."

Mom chuckled.

I kissed them both again and left the house feeling slightly better.

Though we could just be pretending, and really nothing was okay. I knew Dad had a long road ahead of him. Change was hard.

But for now, I was going to hold onto the good. Dad was doing okay. He was in good spirits. And he was willing to take a kale pill if such a beast existed. Those were all things to be happy about.

My apartment was located over the newspaper. The place used to be a rental my parents had for extra income.

Then life with Carson had gone sideways, and now they rented it to me.

I parked LC in my spot and popped in on Stella to see what she needed. She and Dan looked to have things covered, but I told her I would be on hot standby and all she had to do was text. Then I went upstairs, called my sister and calmed her frayed nerves. Afterward, I took a long, hot shower, and had a good cry. Seeing my dad healthy was wonderful and scary. Seeing Catherine had broken my heart, and watching Lora struggle with her grief had been almost too much.

The day had been emotional, and I was exhausted. As much as I hoped Leo and I could find a way to connect tonight, I needed the rest of my day to be low-key. I checked my phone, but no messages from him. I sent a text telling him I was home and to ask him to let me know if he thought he was going to be free later.

After the shower, I blow-dried my hair and then braided it. Dressed in comfy sweats and a T-shirt, I turned on the fire. A fall chill had blown into town, and I was feeling it to my bones. I was shrugging on a hoodie when a knock came at my door. On the other side of the peephole, Leo stood. Had we managed to find time alone together? Standing in the hospital this morning I really didn't think our schedules would line up. I flung open the door.

He held up takeout bags from the local Thai restaurant.

"We did it, sweetness. You and me and some downtime."

I let out a deep sigh of relief. "How great is it that you don't want to get dressed up and go out on the town."

"Nah. Besides, you've had a rough few days, and when I saw you at the ME's office in the hospital, you looked beat."

I moved from the door, so he could enter. He stepped inside and put the takeout bags on the kitchen bar.

I kicked the door closed as I turned to face him.

"I saw my dad today."

"And he's doing okay?" He came toward me, a mysterious smile on his face. I couldn't read what was on his mind. But that was Leo. I hadn't ever really been able to read him. And yet I knew him. Knew he'd always be there for me. Knew he had my back. Knew he would always do the right thing in a situation where the right thing sometimes looked like the wrong thing. Leo was, to his core, one of the good ones.

"Yeah, he's doing okay."

He backed me up until I hit the door and placed his hand on the side of my head. "Then why do you seem ready to leap out of your skin?"

"I just feel unsettled. Like I'm missing something, but I can't figure out what."

He kissed me on the nose. "Maybe you need to blow off some stream. Maybe go for a run or do something to clear your head."

I stuck my hands in the front pockets of his jeans and pulled him toward me. "What might that something be?"

He grinned. "I dunno, got any ideas?" He leaned in closer and brushed a light kiss across my lips.

"Hmm, what could be a good activity for me? I've got a lot of worry and anxiety to work out. Let me list all the things, and you can see just how much of a load I'm under. First, there's my client who was murdered after a likely attempt was made on my other client. And it was supposed to be a simple stalker case. I have a grieving mother who believes her daughter accidentally overdosed, and then—"

He brushed his thumb over my lips. "That's a lot, babe. You've had a crappy week. I'm here to please."

"I think you have the right idea, a run might be just what I need." There was no way I had the energy for a run. But messing with Leo was so much fun.

His smile fell. "Seriously?"

I chuckled. "No way," I tugged him closer and let my body melt against his. I sighed with contentment as he pressed his lips to mine.

Every cell in my body ignited. Yeah, this was exactly what I needed.

"Aw, man," someone said from behind us. "I really didn't want to witness this or what you're planning to follow it up with."

CHAPTER NINE

Carson.

Leo and I didn't move except to end the kiss. Leo rested his forehead on the front door. I looked over his shoulder at Carson standing in the hallway by my bedroom.

"How did you get in?" From the back of my apartment there is a door and a stairway that leads to my dad's newspaper below. When Carson and I were married, we'd lived in a townhouse. I knew he didn't have keys to this place.

"I picked the lock," he said, coming into the living room. He flung himself on the couch, stretching out so he was lying down. "Man, am I beat." He raised his head. "Do I smell pho? Chicken pho, maybe?" His gaze locked on the takeout bags.

"Oh, no you don't," I said. "You can't break in here and then eat our dinner. You weren't invited."

"And is that any way to treat the man who's been living in the trenches, trying to find out about the hit on you?" He yawned.

On closer inspection, his clothes did indeed look lived in

by a few days. Carson's typically shaven face was covered with at least three days of growth, and he was sporting the faded bruises of a black eye.

Dead or alive, Carson was exhausting. When I thought he was dead, I had to deal with all the baggage he'd left behind. Now alive, I had to deal with him. And let's be honest, I had to live with the reminder that one wild weekend in Vegas we'd decided to up our dating game and get married. When a couple makes the six-month mark without major obstacles, of course marriage seemed like a good idea. That was the lie we told ourselves.

I snorted with derision.

"What?" Carson and Leo said in unison.

"What?" I repeated.

"You snorted," Leo said.

Surprised, I asked, "Did I say anything out loud?" Because if my snort had been in my head *and out loud* ,what else had I let slip?

"Thinking bad thoughts about me?" Carson said. He gave me his crooked smile. The same smile that once upon a time I'd found endearing. These days, I found it annoying.

I did some quick mental replaying of the conversation before answering. "I'm thinking that we know there's a hit on me and who put it out there, but didn't that die down when Prescott went to prison?"

I knew my question was a stupid one as soon as it was out of my mouth. I mean, the guy who put the hit out on me —Carson's old business partner, Joe Cooper—did it from prison. The one I sent him to. But I didn't go after him; he came after me. And when I discovered he was wrapped up in a scheme that would affect my hometown, what choice did a girl have except to take down the bad guy? But if he could put a hit out on me from prison once, he could do it again and again and again until a taker was successful. And just because I'd sent his first taker to prison too, well, I supposed that didn't mean there wasn't a second taker waiting in the wings.

I gave Leo a squeeze on the hips, telling him we'd get back to this first chance we got, then stepped away, moving to sink into the club chair next to the couch. "You're saying someone else took the contract on me, aren't you?"

Leo followed and went to the couch shoving Carson on the leg while gesturing for him to sit up. When Carson did, Leo took the seat on the end of the couch closest to me. "We knew arresting Prescott wouldn't make the contract on your life magically go away. What's really bugging you?"

"My dad. It's one thing to know that I could be in danger because of my job. It's another to know someone is hunting me because Cooper put a contract out on me. He can't find out about this."

Leo explained to Carson about my dad's heart attack.

"Sorry about your dad." Carson pinched the bridge of his nose. "I knew Cooper wouldn't let this go. He or some proxy —I'm not sure who yet—posted on a forum. Toby's been tracking the IP address and trying to follow the trail to see where the post originated. If I can prove Cooper did it, we can take legal action. Then two days ago someone accepted the contract. I hit the streets to try to find out who. I had a possible lead that took me to downtown Portland, but"—he gestured to himself— "that didn't pan out."

"Toby has to swear to not tell my dad. But you know the minute we tell him to keep a lid on it, he'll get all nervous and will for sure tell my dad."

Carson grunted and nodded. "I can try and find another

IT guy to help. I trust Toby; that's why I asked him. Hiring this out is gonna cost a pretty penny."

Leo stiffened. "We're talking about Sam's life. Money shouldn't be an obstacle."

Carson raised a brow, "But it could be. Cooper has deep pockets, and if he used a proxy, which I'm guessing he did, then we're out-moneyed."

I raised a hand. "Don't I get a say in this? Since it is my life we're talking about."

Carson nodded. "Of course."

"You and I both know you have lots of money. And I'm positive you made sure you had access to it in your new life before you staged your death."

Carson looked away and cleared his throat. An admission of guilt if I ever saw one.

I continued, "I say we do what it takes when we need to. For now, Toby keeps working it. I trust him, too, and I don't want to try and vet another person. Someone in the black market could double cross us. Let's be mindful what we tell Toby, for Toby's sake. And my dad's."

Carson nodded. He leaned back against the couch and rested his head back, eyes closed. "That food sure smells good."

"Well then, go get yourself some from the restaurant," Leo bit out.

I was frustrated but more embarrassed that I'd been conned by this man. Fell for the whole line about just a regular working Joe in the private security business. Which wasn't exactly a lie. He was in the private security business. A multimillion-dollar operation. But the regular Joe had been a person he'd created, new name and all. He was a piece of fiction, and Carson sitting in my place now, not doing everything in his power to protect me, was proof positive. He loved living on the edge, outwitting people. He was getting a kick from how he was spending his days. The fact that he'd picked the fake surname of Holmes hadn't been a coincidence. Carson loved a good mystery and challenge. And here he was telling me about a hit on my life in the same breath he was asking for food.

I hit my breaking point. I jumped up and grabbed a bag and tossed it to him. "Here, eat already. Finish what you came to say, and get out."

He caught the bag, looking stunned.

"Please," I said. "Get out, *please*. I've had a really bad few days, and you're just adding to it. It's not that I don't appreciate what you're doing. Never mind that I'm in this situation because of you, but regardless, I do appreciate the help. But I need to just forget all of this for a few hours. I need to catch my breath."

Carson looked between me and Leo. He set the bag on the coffee table and stood. "I came to ask you to lie low. Maybe stay inside and keep your blinds drawn until I can figure out who took this contract. I can send you away. Someplace secret where you could work on your tan or something."

I was the palest of whites. I didn't tan. I freckled. I rolled my eyes.

"And you have a lead? Because I thought you said you had nothing." Leo asked. "I can help run things down."

"I don't have a lead, but I expect to have something in the next few days."

"Something might not be the name of the person. Getting that could take days or weeks. The only way to stop this is to go to Cooper. Which you can't do because it'll tip your hand that you're still alive. I'm not going to hole up and hide."

"Then carry a gun. Carry a stun gun. Carry mace. Carry all of it, and limit where you go alone. Be smart. Watch your back." He turned to Leo. "Watch her back."

"I always have." Leo met my eyes. "We've been mindful of a possible contract since Prescott was arrested. We've been cautious. Not much has changed."

I nodded. Letting it all sink in.

Carson moved to stand in my hallway, intending to leave the same way he came in, from the back. "I'll let you know the minute I find out something. If you need me, tell Toby." He then slipped quietly out of my house, leaving the takeout on the coffee table.

CHAPTER TEN

ON MONDAY I TRIED TO START THE WEEK WITH A FRESH mindset. Even though I didn't work a typical workweek, today felt like the start of a new week. And a new week meant endless possibilities. I mean, realistically, every day meant that. I needed to focus on the positive, what I knew and what I could control, and not all the other crap that was stressing me out.

I'd spent the weekend looking over all the photos. I needed more ... everything. There simply were too many pieces missing to solve this puzzle. My first stop was back at Lora and Nessa's house. I was hoping no one would be there this time, and I wanted to do a more thorough search. I had the photos I'd taken of Nessa's journal, but I wanted to get better shots of her room and office, that's why I had brought my camera. My instincts told me something was amiss, like they'd done at the hospital. Only I didn't know what was wrong at the house. Figuring out why I'd been uneasy at the hospital had been a no-brainer ... both women getting sick on the same night wasn't a coincidence.

Though Lora had given me the go-ahead to pursue Nessa's death as a murder, no one else was on board with the idea. And Lora herself spent the majority of the day cycling through her grief. I couldn't burden her with any undue issues, thoughts, or concerns. I was going to have to rely heavily on my team of Toby, Leo, and Precious for this case. I'd relied heavily on them in the past, and as a PI trying to build a career, I'd wanted to not always have to depend on them. I had hoped this case would be the one where I would need them less. Who was I kidding. From the minute I took this case and we decided to use Precious's business as part of my ruse, I'd already burdened my friends too much.

From all appearances, Nessa and Lora's house looked empty. I parked a few houses down anyway and made my way to the garage door. I used the access code Lora had given me while in the hospital, the one that was supposed to open the front door. I keyed in the five digits, and the lock disengaged. So one code for all access points. I was stunned Walt hadn't changed this. So much seemed off about this case.

I eased the door open but didn't enter. I stared at the keypad. I suppose having the same code at any door was to be expected. Yet... one code for everyone? There was no telling who came and went in this house. Part of the perk of the keyless entry was to assign people a code and to allow access at certain times only. Without that, Lora and Nessa's house was a free-for-all.

On a whim, I called Lason Dell at Click and Shop. He'd been here delivering groceries the day I'd come to meet everyone. I crossed my fingers that he was working. He answered on the third ring.

I'd worked a case when I first became a PI where I had to

investigate Lason. I could comfortably say he was one of the nicest guys I'd ever met.

"Click and Shop, this is Lason. How can I help you?"

"Hey Lason, it's Samantha True, how are you?"

"Doing fine, Sam. I hope you're calling to say you want to pick up some shifts. We are understaffed and overcooked. We could use your help."

"I wish I could, Lason. I'm feeling a little overcooked myself. My dad had a heart attack the other day, and I'm not sure if you heard this or not, but that house where you delivered groceries a few days ago, the one where we ran into each other—"

"Yeah, the mochi house."

"Yeah, well, one of the women who lived there was killed. I'm working that case."

"Jeez, Sam, that's awful. Was it the one I met?"

"No. I'm calling about your visit here, actually. I think the women who lived here regularly had Click and Shop deliver, and I was wondering if you could look into their accounts, I can give you their names. Just tell me if they left a key code to the garage so the groceries could be left there." This wasn't unusual for people to do. That practice was stunning to me, stunningly stupid, to be frank.

"You know I can't tell you the code, Sam." He sounded put off.

I didn't bother to remind him that I was technically still an employee and could come in and look up the account myself. Another scary truth.

I said, "I don't need the code. I have it. I'm just wondering if they gave it out and if it's the same code. I'm trying to determine if people other than the residents had it."

"Oh, gotcha. And I'd be helping with this case, trying to

right the wrong for that young lady?" Still uncertain, but a tad more willingness came through in his voice.

"Yeah, you would. And she wasn't much younger than us, Lason. Maybe ten years. Too young to die for sure."

"Okay, give me the name and address."

I did and listened to the clacking of the keyboard.

He cleared his throat. "Okay. I see it. And yeah, there's a code entered here."

"Is it two-two-zero-two-six?" Again, I wasn't asking him to tell me the code, just to verify.

"Uh, yeah."

I sighed wearily. "Lason, do you have keyless entry on your house?"

"Yeah, why?"

"Do you have it set up correctly, where every person gets their own code, and you can permit access at various times of the week and day?"

"Sorta. Marni made me give my mom her own code. And she can't have access at night." Marni was Lason's girlfriend and a former client of mine. I had, in fact, done a background check on him as she was gun shy when it came to trusting her heart with men.

I smiled, even though he'd basically told me he was no better at using this tool than Nessa and Lora. "Well, maybe you should think about setting it up properly. I'm looking at a tool that could help me solve what I think is a murder ... had it been used correctly."

Lason's gasp came through the line. "Will do, Sam. And if you think you need a break from that stress, come here, please. Get some of our stress."

I chuckled. "Thanks, I'll let you know if I can help."

We said our goodbyes, and I slid my phone in my

messenger bag. I took the lens off my camera and entered the garage. It was empty. I went to the garbage bin and lifted the lid. It was empty as well. I took pictures of both the garage and the garbage can then went to the door that led into the house. Another keyless entry. I entered the same code, and the door unlocked.

Words could not express my irritation, though the cause of it was a moot point.

Inside the butler's pantry, the hum of the freezer was the only sound. The space was as clean as it had been the other day, and it was eerily quiet. I eased the door shut. Natural light lit the house, and I made my way from the pantry to the kitchen. I opened the fridge. Only products with a long shelf life had remained. I took pictures. Same for the freezer. The recycling was empty as well.

My best guess was Lora and Nessa had been poisoned through food. And since they both ate the ice cream and drank the tea before the game, I believe those had been the vessels to deliver the poison.

But all evidence of any food they'd had that night was long gone.

A sense of unease creeped over me. I went into both Nessa's and Lora's offices and took pictures. I opened drawers, flipped through calendars, and looked for hidden compartments. I was disappointed not to find any. Nessa's purse was hanging on a coatrack by the front door. I dumped it out on the floor and took pictures. There was nothing in her wallet or purse pockets that could be helpful. I didn't find her cell phone and assumed her mother had it.

Upstairs, I did the same in their rooms. More so in Nessa's, taking lots of pictures of the medicine cabinet and bedside table with the journal.

Her medicine journal was right where I'd left it. After donning latex gloves, I pulled it out and flipped through it again. I took more pictures of the week leading up to her death. I had these on my phone, but I liked extras; part of me was always worried about losing the originals. I was putting the book away when the corner of a paper poked out from the back pages.

I hadn't seen this page before, so I pulled it out and unfolded the sheet.

Reading typed work was easier if the font used was wide and heavy on the bottom. Being a dyslexic had gotten easier as technology improved. This note was done in an easy-to-read font.

Stunned by what I was reading, I placed the sheet on the bed and took photos.

If this page was authentic, then it was a typed good-bye letter from Nessa.

I squatted by the bed and stared at the page. I was curious whose prints might be on it, and was glad I had donned gloves. Would Nessa's prints be there? Possibly mine, since I had touched the journal the other day. If only I could I take it and find out.

If I was right about Nessa's death and I took this letter, then it couldn't be used as evidence later. Man, I'd kill to be able to look for prints right here and now.

My vibrating phone interrupted my thoughts. The thread of this case was falling apart in my mind and spreading in all directions from the interruption.

I pulled up my phone and glanced at the screen. Toby.

"Hey."

"Sam, where are you?"

"I'm at Lora's house."

He sounded panicked. "Can you turn on the TV?"

I glanced around even though I was alone. It still felt wrong. "Just tell me what's going on."

"Nessa's mom is on the local TV station's morning talk show. And she is bashing the heck out of you and Precious."

I fell back on my butt. Forgetting all about the letter on the bed.

"What? What do you mean bashing the heck out of us?"

"First, she talked about accidental overdoses and how parents can help monitor their kids' medicines to try to make sure something like this doesn't happen again. She warned about the dangers of Warfarin. No big deal, right? Then, she went on to say how Nessa had been doing fine. She had just graduated with her business degree and was excited about what she could do with her business. But then Lora convinced her to hire a life coach, implying that her life needed to be improved. She said as soon as the life coach entered Lora and Nessa's lives, Nessa mixed up her medicines. It's like this life coach got in Nessa's head. Took her focus off what mattered and put the focus on something else. That doing all this had made her daughter behave differently. She said that right up to the day Nessa died, she was agitated and combative. She implied we did this to Nessa."

"Did they name Precious or me specifically? The company specifically?"

"Yep and put pictures up too. And they mentioned that Precious is also the life coach for AJ who had been arrested last year for the murder of Keith McVay. And how he was the best quarterback the Portland Pioneers ever had, and blah blah blah. Oh, and of course, the conspiracy theorists are chiming in."

Oh crap. "Have you been able to get in touch with Precious?"

I needed to call her ASAP.

"She's not picking up."

"Okay. I'll try now. I think we'll need to meet at my house. We need to review this case, because things aren't adding up properly. This isn't good at all."

"Sounds solid, but watch your back. Because the heat has started to roll in from social media. And I'm guessing having your picture flashed across a lot of screens saying that you work for Precious isn't a good thing, considering the stuff that Carson's having me look into."

"Nope, not a good thing at all." I sighed wearily.

We disconnected, and I sat there in silence for a few moments, trying to put the pieces together. To figure out a plan. To figure out why Catherine would go after us.

The last thing I wanted was to bring Precious's company into the spotlight negatively. But soon with my picture on the screen, people were going to start putting two and two together, and social media was going to realize that I'm a private investigator.

No telling how Catherine would feel about that.

I stood, antsy to leave, but had to clean up. I tucked the note back in the journal and returned it to the nightstand. If this was evidence, it would need to be found and taken in by the police. I paused when I heard the telltale creak of someone coming up the stairs.

CHAPTER ELEVEN

I slid my phone quietly into my messenger bag and withdrew my stun gun. I paused to listen before padding quietly across the carpeted room. Leaning near the door I strained to pick up the quiet sounds of the intruder.

Another creak on the stairs.

I flicked the stun gun on. There were two options. One would be to wait and see who came around the corner. The other to try to evade them and slip out undetected. The way the person was creeping up the stairs made me think they knew I was here, but I couldn't be sure of that.

Blowing out a slow, steady breath helped calm my nerves. I considered the weapon in my hand, wondering if I was bringing a stun gun to a gun or knife fight. I hoped for a knife.

I peeked out of the room toward the stairs, aware I could be tipping off my presence. Caleb the stalker was on the landing, his hand on the newel post, his head cocked at an angle that told me he was listening for something too.

"Caleb!" I exited Nessa's room. "What are you doing here?"

Startled, his mouth flapped open like a fish out of water. He made a sound as if he wanted to say something, but instead took a few steps backwards before turning to fly down the stairs. His steps thundered as he leapt down two at a time.

"Caleb!" I ran after him, skipping stairs as well, using the handrail to balance me. I was almost on him when he juked to the right and cut across the kitchen, putting the island between us. He faced me, but not before grabbing a knife from the knife block on the counter.

Remind me to be mad at the universe later for granting that particular wish but not some of my other better ones.

He swung the knife wildly in front of him in a crazy eight pattern, getting off track to jab it at me every few beats.

Clutched in my hand was my stun gun, and I raised it too, so he knew I was armed. I made it crackle and pop a few times for good measure.

"How did you get in here?" I asked.

"I used the code. It's not hard to figure out. It's either someone's birthday, or something like the year they started making money, or the year they had the first million subscribers. Which, by the way that's what it is: year plus month. I know when that is because they made a whole YouTube video to celebrate the achievement, but they did it in reverse."

"Reverse?"

"They filmed it regular but loaded it in reverse. So I took the date and plugged it in backwards and that's how I got it. I figured I had like seven options, and I nailed it on the fourth try."

"Okay. Now tell me why you're here?" I wave my stun gun and made it spark again. "Start talking."

He curled up his lip and mimicked me with a knife wave of his own. "I think I should talk to nobody. I came to warn Lora."

"Lora isn't here, and you already warned her at the hospital. You scared her. Why were you creeping up the stairs?" I waved my stun gun in the direction of the stairs. "Did you come to warn her, or did you come to do to her what you did to Nessa?"

Caleb gasped.

"Yeah, it was an awful thing to say, but is it true?"

Caleb was short and stocky with long legs but a stubby torso. Even with him holding the knife, I figured I could take him. But I didn't want to. And the way he tossed the knife from hand to hand told me he was confident in his ability.

I pushed forward with the interrogation. "Let's try again. Came to warn Lora about what?"

"She's in danger."

"From whom? Because to me, it looks like you're the one posing the most threat."

"Maybe from you. You broke into their house too. I heard what Nessa's mom said on the TV. Maybe you did this to them."

"I have permission to be here. I was actually given the code to get in. But I'm not who you came to warn Lora about, am I? You broke in here—"

"It's not breaking in when you know the code." He raised a brow, daring me to argue back.

I couldn't really because I'd used that same defense in the past.

Taking advantage of my pause, Caleb lurched toward

the island while simultaneously grabbing an orange. He threw the knife across the counter and chucked the orange at me.

"Hey!" I ducked.

The first orange sailed over me. A second caught me in the shoulder. A third in the chest. I was swinging my arms madly trying to swat oranges out of the sky.

Next thing I knew, the bowl that held the oranges came flying over. I ducked, covering my head as the ceramic bowl shattered against the floor, and tiny ceramic pieces sprayed everywhere. Caleb sprinted past me and out the kitchen door to the garage. I quickly followed, crossed but he had a few yards on me.

Once outside the garage, he jumped on a bicycle and pedaled furiously away, looking over his shoulder every few seconds.

I stopped chasing him, but not because I was winded. I was confident I could catch up with him. He was headed in the same direction of where LC was parked, so even if I couldn't catch him on foot, I could with LC. But Caleb didn't seem like the most pressing issue. Maybe he was weird. And maybe he had crossed a line or two, but the guy opted to chuck oranges at me instead of coming at me with a knife. Besides, he wasn't going anywhere far on that bike.

Right now? Right now, I had to know what kind of damage Catherine had done to Precious's business. And knowing I was working for Lora was gonna tell the hit man how to find me. That wasn't good either.

I sent texts to Toby, Precious, and Leo and asked them to meet me at my apartment in an hour, and I promised food. Following a quick stop at the Mexican food truck where I picked up an assortment of street tacos, chips, salsa, guacamole, and nachos, I headed home. It was a crappy day, which called for comfort food. I knew I needed some, and I was confident Precious could use them too. Toby always needed comfort food.

Precious was the first to show up. She was dressed in a dark-gray power suit, a coach's whistle hung around her neck. Her pale-blonde hair was in a French twist, and for all intents and purposes, she looked great, calm, as if nothing was wrong. But at second glance, I knew she'd been crying. Her lashes were devoid of mascara, and her cheeks lacked color. I'm guessing she was mainlining Visine to hide her bloodshot eyes.

I pulled her into a hug. "I'm sorry. What can I do? Do you want me to release a statement saying that I wasn't working for you, that it was a ruse? That I'm a PI? Because I will."

She hugged me back, then pulled away, shaking her head. "I don't really know what to do yet. And I don't believe in making decisions in the heat of the moment. Right now, I'm very emotional, and that's not going to help me determine the right decision. The personal attacks online are just disgusting." She held out her phone. "You should see my email. Some are supportive, others are filled with hate and threats. If this is what Lora and Nessa went through with their stalker, my heart breaks for them because I just have to say ... it's scary. They handled it way better than I'm handling it right now."

My best friend since third grade took a seat at the counter, peeled off her suit coat, dropped it to the floor, then helped herself to some nachos.

Toby busted in as I was picking up Precious's coat. Hanging from around his neck like a jumbo pendant was a felt grapefruit the size of a soccer ball. Inside the felt fruit shape's pouch was his emotional support animal, a sugar glider named Lady M. Her small fuzzy head peeked out the top of the pouch. Toby stroked the head with his thumb. I scratched her head, too. She cooed, and I understood why Toby relied on her; my own blood pressure dropped with her sound. Toby slung his laptop bag into the chair next to my couch and beelined straight for the nachos.

"As I see it," he said, his mouth half-full. "The sooner we wrap this up, the sooner we go back to normal. I will never complain about boring insurance claims again. I thought I wanted high-profile cases, but I've changed my mind. Juggling these two cases is stressing me right out. I don't like Nessa's mom. I'm trying to be understanding, even sympathetic, but it's hard. When she threw you both in the spotlight and was, like, painting giant bull's-eyes on you both. Well, Sam already has a bull's-eye, except maybe now hers are neon and flashing."

Precious looked at me. "Bull's-eyes?"

"The hit. We've learned it's still active."

Precious closed her eyes and pulled in a deep breath through her nose. This was her way of gathering herself.

We gave her the moment she needed. When she was done, less than a minute later, she turned to Toby and reached for a chip. "As for Nessa's mom, you don't have to understand. Just accept that she's grieving, and that Sam and I are able to weather her. It's not personal. She'd attack anyone in our place." Precious scooped a glob of guacamole up and shoved it in her mouth.

"Now that we're all on the same page with the hit, you'll understand if I put some distance between us." In hindsight, maybe I shouldn't have any of my friends over. I didn't want anybody to be caught in the crossfire. Protecting them was as important to me as reducing my dad's stress.

"As if," Precious said. "All you have to do is call, and we'll be there."

I nodded once, a lump in my throat from her words. I was so lucky to have these people in my life. Needing a second to gather myself, I reached behind the couch and pulled out a giant Post-it note board. I ripped off several sheets, then pressed them to the wall. This was our standard way of reviewing the case. Sometimes seeing it out in writing, and making something of a murder board really helped us organize our thoughts and gave us a plan.

Precious took the guacamole bowl in one arm and picked up a marker in the other. "I know you're hiding something from me. You'll spill soon enough."

I dipped a chip in her guac. "You have enough on your plate."

She nodded. "I'll write." She moved to the Post-it notes on the wall. On the first page, she wrote INCIDENT.

I began, "Both Lora and Nessa ate the same food the night of the game. Lora started before she got online. Nessa while she was online. Lora immediately started having a bad stomachache, and she thought the symptoms could be related to her ulcer. I took her to the doctor. Toby, what did you see with Nessa?"

He sat on the couch and cuddled Lady M. "It was awful, really. And happened so suddenly. She was gaming, chatting. At first, she was energetic. But then she seemed to slow down. I thought it was normal for her. That she was getting her groove. A few times she mumbled something, and I wondered if she was just concentrating. Addie came into the room, asked her if she wanted something and touched her shoulder. Nessa slumped forward and asked for help. Then she fell out of the chair. Addie called nine-one-one. I couldn't see anything at that point because they were on the floor, but I heard Addie tell the operator that Nessa wasn't breathing."

I'd seen someone die from poisoning. That event was a slideshow in my brain I relived from time to time. Toby would have this experience too. I squeezed his hand.

To Precious, I said, "Both Nessa and Lora ate mochi and drank boba tea. I don't think they touched the other food. Nessa was dead on arrival when she got to the hospital. The autopsy showed that she overdosed on her heart medicine, Warfarin. Lora's toxicology screen showed she also had the Warfarin in her system. That's what triggered her ulcer to start bleeding."

Precious turned to me. "You're saying they were poisoned?"

"It looks that way."

She wrote POISONED on the paper, then moved to the next sheet.

She wrote SUSPECTS and underlined it before facing me.

"The first suspect is Addie Milner. She's Nessa's and Lora's assistant. She's the one who bought the boba tea, served the mochi, and was putting the other food together. I also found her the day after Nessa died, cleaning the house. All the food items had been removed and thrown away."

"Well, duh," Toby said. "She sounds like a no-brainer. We should just have Leo go arrest her."

"On what grounds? The medical examiner is saying that Nessa died from an accidental overdose of prescribed medication, which is what Nessa's mom has told the media as well. The day after Nessa died, I spoke with PI Walt. He seemed to think suicide could be a possibility. But to say that out loud would destroy Catherine, so they're happy to accept accidental overdose, because obviously, the alternative is worse." I grabbed my camera from where I'd stowed it by the front door and switched to the playback mode. "But here's something weird. Earlier today, I was at Nessa's house, and I found her journal. It's where she logs when she takes her pills, when she gets her prescription filled, other meds she had to take in case it counteracts with her prescription, and any side effects she might be having. Meticulous is an understatement. Inside that journal was a suicide note. Typed, not signed."

Precious shook her head. "Nope, I'm not buying it."

I showed them the pictures and sent the images to my printer. "I don't believe it either."

"Next suspect?" Precious stood with pen poised.

"Caleb Harris. He's the man Walt identified as their stalker. In Walt's file, he'd printed out several online threads where Caleb has gotten combative and made what could be seen as threats. That is, if you read his post without reading the entire thread." I pointed at Toby. "My mom will kill you if she knows you're giving my dad work, but good thing you did because when read in context, his posts are ugly, sure, but they are in defense of people. Immature, sure. But he never threatens anyone's life or livelihood specifically. The ones highlighted by Walt are Caleb saying people will get theirs and paybacks are hell. He could be talking about karma for all I know."

Precious held up a finger. "But didn't you say he was at the hospital the night Nessa died? Explain that?"

"I can't, yet. He was very agitated, and when I walked in,

it did sound like he was threatening her. But Lora was more bothered by his agitation than his words. I had a run-in with him today. He chose to throw oranges at me instead of using the knife in his hand. I want to rule him out, but his inconsistency is why he's on the suspect list. I also want to know how he knew about Nessa before I did, before Toby called me to tell me she collapsed and was on the way to the hospital."

Toby chimed in. "I've been going through their messages and chats and games and jumping in on different gaming forums. These girls have a big-time enemy in the gaming world. From what I've gathered, the gamer tag *"all fired up"* belongs to Winnie Dunlap. Sam's dad found some news articles about how Winnie was being considered for the same sponsorship that Lora is up for with that kids' streaming service. But Winnie posted a few videos that upset parents: something about some bad words in a handful of her videos, and online accusations about unethical gaming. She's cleaned up her act a lot, but you know the internet is forever. All that surfaced when the network was looking into her. That's when they shifted to Nessa and Lora. Those two are —were—squeaky clean. Wholesome. Winnie accused them of doxing her."

"Did they?" I asked. Telling the network about Winnie's past was a dirty move.

Toby shrugged. "Hard to say, the leaks were anonymous. But it doesn't really matter because any IT person hired by the network could have found these videos and threads about Winnie. Took your dad seconds."

"My dad is a good researcher."

"The info was on the second page of a Google search."

Together, Precious and I "ahhed" in understanding.

"That's why I think this Winnie Dunlap should be on

our list. Losing out on hundreds of thousands of dollars is motive enough for me." Toby stuffed a taco in his mouth.

A rap on my door interrupted any further conversation. I checked the peephole, as if a contract killer would knock. You never know. Thankfully, it was Leo, and with him was Paulie Bea.

Paulie Bea was short, squatty, frank, and awesome. He lifted a hand in greeting. "So this is where the masterminds meet to solve crime." His eyes went large when he saw the food on the bar. "And food. Count me in." He grabbed a plate and started loading it.

I gave Leo an inquisitive look. I had no objection to Paulie being here. He was my PI mentor, after all. Leo had brought us together. Typically, we met at the dog park where he usually hung out with his giant schnauzer, Rocket, now that he'd retired from the business. Thanks to Paulie Bea, I had the insurance gigs that I did. I was simply surprised Leo would bring another person into the fold when he knew there was a hit out on me.

He met my gaze with a solid stare. "With his years of experience, he might see something we didn't." I nodded and moved back to the Post-it notes.

"Paulie, this is where we try to think through everything and hope to put together a picture."

After loading his plate, he stared at my Post-it boards while shoving food in his face. After a few bites be paused. "Heard you took a case Walt Adler was already on."

"Yeah, Lora and Nessa hired me because they thought Walt wasn't really looking into any other people besides Caleb as their stalker. They wanted me to see if he missed something."

Paulie's brows went up. "That couldn't have gone over

well. I know Walt. He's a good guy. Took a defensive-driving class from him that has saved my bacon more times than I can count, but he is not one to share very well."

"My clients asked me not to tell him."

His chin lifted in understanding. "Ah, that makes sense now. Explains why the media is saying you were a life-coach assistant. You know, it's only a matter of time before the truth comes out?"

I dreaded that day. I really hadn't seen this case going sideways and had hoped no one but Nessa and Lora would be the wiser with me taking this case. But Paulie was right. The fact that I took a case that would essentially prove a colleague wrong would be whispered about me in professional circles for years to come.

I lifted one shoulder in a dismissive shrug. "That goes on my list of low-level worries. I've got this to get through first." I made a sweeping gesture to the boards.

Paulie scanned our murder board. "You're going to need a second murder board. Maybe over there." He pointed to an opposite wall. "You need to separate the cases."

"Separate the cases?" Precious asked. "We're not counting defaming my business as a case, right?" Disgruntled, she sat in the armchair with a plop. "I know that's not what you mean about another murder board, but I feel like I have a case against the mom. If only she wasn't grieving, I'd do something about it."

Guilt swamped me. Had I made Precious's company the target by having that exchange with Catherine at the park, or maybe it was something I said to Walt. For every action, there is a reaction. I just wish I knew which of my actions had caused it.

Paulie wiped guacamole off his chin. "I mean I don't think the stalking and murder are connected."

I spun to face him. "Me either. And I think the girls were right. I think they have a stalker, and it's not Caleb. Or there's someone else besides Caleb. I just don't think Caleb has escalated to the point of murder."

I recapped for Leo and Paulie what I'd said earlier about Caleb, including my run-in with him at Lora's house.

Paulie shook his head. "I know I told you to trust your gut, but stalkers are tricky. They run good cons on all sorts of people."

"That's just it. He's not the con type. He's too flustered. Too...disorganized."

"Not enough." Paulie shook his head. "And you're gonna need to put the third Post-it board on a different wall. You're running out of space, girl. You can't afford any more trouble. A murder, a stalker, and a contract on your life. That's a lot to juggle in one week." Paulie chuckled and pointed at my door. "Just stick it on the back of the door."

I looked to Leo for him to explain why he'd told Paulie.

"Tell her how you know about the contract, Paulie," Leo said.

"Heck, it's all anyone on the street can talk about. The money is big, huge, and now there's a ticking clock. There's a six-figure bonus if someone gets you in the next two days."

"How do you eat an elephant?" my dad always asked.

One bite at a time.

We'd decided last night that Precious would put out a statement about how she and her company were sorry for the loss of Vanessa Taylor, and though a life coach did look at all aspects of a person's life and any medical issues or concerns were always discussed with the medical provider at the center of the discussion, neither Precious nor representatives from her company had ever had any such discussions with Vanessa Taylor with or without her medical provider.

Our goal was to halt the bleeding before it got out of control. Precious considered hiring a crisis management PR team, but was hesitant as the expense could wipe her out, and what was the point, when it was all said and done, if she were bankrupt?

I decided to get to the bottom of Caleb once and for all. Right now, he was on the hook for stalking Lora and Nessa, and he'd made some statements that had me uncomfortable. I figured he'd be the easiest of my avenues to pursue.

Caleb lived in an apartment near the interstate and on the edge of Wind River. He was within walking distance of the town's grocery store and a few chain restaurants.

I climbed the stairs to his third-floor apartment and rapped on his door, placing a finger over his peephole. If he saw me, he'd never open the door.

"Who's there?" he called through the thin door.

"I work for Lora Darling. Are you aware that Lora has a stalker and currently you are suspected of being that person?" Sometimes the truth worked best.

Silence. I waited him out.

"Why are you covering my peephole?"

"I'm going to uncover it now. And I'm going to hold up my ID. My name is Sam. I'm a private investigator that was hired by Lora and Nessa. I only want to talk with you." The minute he saw my face he'd probably remember my stun gun and would likely tell me to go pound sand.

I replaced my finger with my PI license, which included a photo.

"Wait a sec," he protested.

I removed my ID to let him see me. "Yeah, I was there yesterday. I was also there at the hospital. You saw me with Lora. You said something that night that has stuck with me."

"What?"

His voice was close to the door making me think he was leaning on it.

"You said she needed to be careful, that she was next."

"Sounds kinda bad if you thought I was stalking her."

"Yeah, it does, but Caleb, I didn't hear it as a threat. I

heard it as a warning. That you might know something that we don't. That you're trying to protect Lora."

A latch clicked, and he eased the door open a crack. "I would do anything to protect both of them. They're... they were my friends."

I gestured to the space behind him. "Do you think I can come in? I want you to tell me all about your friendship with Lora and Nessa. I need to know everything from your side."

He opened the door farther and stuck his head out, looking all around me. "Were you followed?"

I looked around too. "I don't think so."

Truth is, I should know the answer to that for sure. Especially as there's a hit out on my life. Either I was slipping, or I was the worst PI in the business. Being this careless was not how a person stayed alive.

"There's a man who hides in the shadows and watches me. He might be watching you too."

I looked around again, this time paying more attention. *Note to self:* find out if Caleb had any mental health issues.

"Okay," Caleb said. "I don't see him. Come on in." He flung the door open and gestured wildly for me to hurry and enter. Once I did, he slammed the door behind me. "That dude gives me the creeps."

"What does he look like?" I took in his apartment. Typical guy place. Couch, big TV, and in one corner, a large desk with several monitors and a computer tower that was glowing green.

"I've never seen his face. He's always wearing a hat and stays in the shadows. I call him The Shadow Man."

"How do you know he's there for you and not someone else?"

Caleb was silent, so I turned toward him.

"Because I've seen him other places, like when I'm out to eat."

"He follows you?"

He shrugged. "I guess. I'm not that hard to follow. I don't have a car, so I stick to this area mostly."

I nodded in understanding. Hence the bike yesterday. I pointed to the computer. "You game?"

"Yep. That's how I met Nessa and Lora. It was years ago, like, their senior year in high school. I was in college. I was kinda lonely, so I was gaming a lot. I'd been in some games where they played. Then there was a convention in town that they were at, so I went. I met them in person, and the next time we were playing *Shadow Walker,* they let me join their team. They were super nice, and we did well, so they let me join again. Lora's brothers were playing, too, and the four of them were giving each other a hard time and laughing. They were having fun, and so was I."

Caleb didn't strike me as the type to have lots of friends. And based on how active he was on social media, I figured that was his community. Lora and Nessa were his tribe. "You've been gaming with them for a couple years now?"

"Close to three. I've been a fan for five."

"They give you a hard time when you play?"

He smiled. "Yeah. For sure. It's awesome."

Just as I thought: Caleb saw Nessa and Lora as family. "Any new people join the team recently?" I needed to find a reason Caleb would feel his place among the team was threatened.

"No, they're pretty selective. If you aren't nice online, then they won't invite you in."

I recalled the post Caleb had made in the past. "That

can't be true. No offense, but you have said some ugly things online. Am I wrong?"

His ducked his head, a red stain rushing up his cheeks. "No, you aren't wrong. But all that was before I got invited to play. That time I met Lora and Nessa, they said they knew who I was, seen some of my posts. They told me that I seemed like a nice guy in person but not so nice online, and as much as they'd like to hang online, they had to think of Lora's brothers and the message it would send to them if Lora befriended mean people. So I cleaned up my act. I never made an ugly post after that. And trust me, I wanted to. That Winnie Dunlap can be infuriating." His fists balled up at his sides. "You want a stalker, check her. She hated Lora."

"What makes you say Winnie?"

"A lot of my hate posts were directed at her. She would always bash Lora any chance she got."

"And you were defending her?" I knew this, having read the post. This was why context was everything. Though I hadn't realized Winnie had been the target. Sometimes with reading, details escaped me.

He nodded.

I could easily see how he got spun up and struck out verbally after reading trash talk about Lora or Nessa.

"You've been a good friend to them," I said.

He sank onto his couch and swiped a palm across his eyes. "That's how I knew something was wrong with Nessa. She let me join the team that night, and we were about to do a raid. Normally, right before we do one, Nessa always says, 'Okay boys, no man gets left behind.' That's her rule. It's team first, winning second. But we were at the gate, ready to go in, and her character was just standing there. I asked her if she was okay, and she just said my name. They never say our real names. But she did. She said Caleb. And that was it. And I knew something was wrong. That it was bad. I just knew. So I flipped to the online feed and saw her collapse. The only thing I could do was call nine-one-one."

"You called for help?"

He nodded. "And they were too late. I think I knew that too. By the way Addie was screaming Nessa's name."

"Do you mind if I look?" I gestured to his gaming system. He gestured for me to go ahead.

The monitor emitted a calming green glow. I tried to picture the scene unfolding in front of Caleb. Does a stalker call emergency response for his victims? I could easily verify if he was indeed the caller. Caleb could have gotten into the house and poisoned the food. He knew the code, even if he did seem to have just figured it out yesterday. That could all be a ruse.

I glanced around the gaming space for notes or something else to help me. In his trash can, I saw two large empty boba teas.

"You drink boba tea?"

He nodded. "The girls got me hooked on it."

The nearest boba tea shop was easily twenty miles away. "How do you get there? Have it delivered?" I was looking for another thread to follow. Maybe a delivery driver who could verify an alibi? Or not.

"Addie brings it to me."

I pointed to the trash can. "When did she bring those to you? The night of the game?"

He nodded.

So Caleb had drinks from the same place on the same night as Lora and Nessa, but he didn't get sick. This also meant he had access to the girls' drinks before Addie brought them home. Addie seemed to be my common denominator of late.

"You know Addie through Lora and Nessa I'm assuming?"

Again he nodded. "Yeah, we're friends too. But I only got to know her from when I went to the conventions. She's super nice and helpful. She makes sure the gifts I send to Nessa and Lora get to them. You know they get a lot of gifts that they just have to give away. Addie makes sure mine aren't in that pile. And she always emails me to tell me when Lora and Nessa are gonna be at an event because she knows I like to go to those. Sometimes we meet for dinner." He looked out his front window toward the chain restaurants and the grocery store.

I moved to look out the window. "Does Addie live nearby?"

"In those apartments on the other side of the grocery store." He came to stand next to me. "Those. She's building B, third floor like me. That's her balcony."

I found the large B marking the building and tried to follow where he was pointing. "The one on the end?"

"Yep."

"Wow, you guys could use flashlights to communicate." I pictured them both doing a series of messages with Morse code. Precious and I would have totally done something like that.

On the corner of the grocery store, I noticed a camera facing Caleb's apartment entrance. I also noticed one facing his parking lot where there were lots of shadows, a good place for a shadow man to cloak himself.

He laughed. "I never thought of that. I don't even know

if I own a flashlight. To tell you the truth, I never thought she'd stay in the apartment as long as she did. I thought she'd move into the house with Lora and Nessa, but I guess they never asked."

And just like that Caleb gave me Addie's motive.

CHAPTER THIRTEEN

From Caleb's apartment, I went straight to the grocery store, hoping I could talk to the manager and maybe get a copy of the security tapes. That is, if the store kept their security records for longer than twenty-four hours. If the video filmed over itself every day, then I wasn't going to have much luck. I'd have to watch these every day, and only if the manager would share them with me, which by itself was a long shot.

I stood at the customer service desk waiting for someone for five minutes before a young man, with longish hair, a hawkish nose, and a name badge that read Bogey, showed up.

"Can I help you?" he asked while rifling through drawers looking for something.

"Hi, my name is Sam, and a friend of mine has been having some problems at their apartment. They live at the ones right over there." I pointed in the direction of Caleb's place.

Bogey started shaking his head, but I pressed on.

"Someone is hanging around outside bothering them. I

was wondering if it would be possible to look at your security tapes because the camera on this store's north corner faces his apartment directly. We were hoping maybe we could see something, and then we could go to the police."

"No can do, lady. Got to have a warrant to get a look at those security tapes. Just go file a complaint or something. Come back with the police and look at them."

A warrant wasn't going to be remotely possible. There was nothing here for the police to investigate. I considered my options. Would Bogey comply if he thought I was one step below the police. His quick response to doing what he likely thought was legally correct made me rule out offering him money.

Deciding to go with I'm-kinda-like-the-police-but-not-really, I pulled out my private investigator license and the badge I'd bought online and put them on the counter.

"I'm a PI. I have a client who's being stalked. You possibly have the answer to my problem. I'm not asking for copies of the tape. I just want to look at what's on your security feed."

Bogey shook his head. "Nope. Do you think I'm just gonna share somebody's information based on a story you could have just made up. I'm not studying law in school, but I'm saying people on those videos have rights too. You can't come in here like Johnny Law, flash a pseudo badge, and think I'm just gonna do what you want. 'Cause I'm not. People have rights. I have rights." He was like a broken record with everyone's rights.

I slid my badge off the counter and took a step back. This was going sideways, fast.

"Are you the manager?" I'd worked at a grocery store, and standard procedure was to get a manager for a situation like this. What were the chances this kid was the store manager? Low.

He crossed arms. "I'm the assistant manager for today."

Great. "And tomorrow?"

He smirked. "Probably."

"Is there a manager I could talk to?"

"Yeah, but you're gonna have to call, because he's up at the district office. He won't be back for two weeks. He'll tell you what I'm telling you. Come back with a warrant."

Dead end.

"Okay." I wasn't willing to burn this bridge. Not yet at least. "I appreciate your time. Thanks for listening." Even though he kind of really didn't listen, but whatever. Who was I to squeeze a kid into compliance? "One last question; how long does the store keep video footage from your cameras?"

"That's none of your business," he said with a lift of his nose.

Which I took to mean he didn't know.

I went outside and took a moment to stand on the corner facing Caleb's apartment. The camera really did have a good line of sight. I whipped out my phone and took pictures of the camera. Zooming in and trying to find a label or make. I could at least find out if the camera offered quality night vision. For all I knew, the image could be grainy and dark, and getting the video would be useless anyway. I sent the images to Toby before I called.

"It's bad, Sam. Real bad." His immediate agitation caught me off guard.

"What? Those cameras?" I looked around wondering what else he could be talking about.

"Social media. Things have really hit the fan since

Catherine's interview." The rustle of a bag and the following crunching of chips came through the line loud and clear.

A quick glance at my watch showed I had not called Toby during high time. No, this sounded like stress eating. The rate of crunching was coming in fast, almost maniacally.

High time was when Toby clocked out to binge-watch TV, get stoned, and eat a lot of food. This fell between working for me and his time as a private driver and, apparently, calls to my father.

"You sound stressed."

"Dudette, you have no idea. Precious is here. She went to your place, but you weren't home." His voice was low. "She's pacing. I don't know if I've ever seen her pace."

"Pacing means she's having trouble working something out. And I'm guessing it has to do with the social media stuff."

"Ya think?" Toby snorted, then crunched some more. "She's getting vilified online. It's awful. But that's not the worst right now. You're at the grocery store right now, aren't you?"

"Yeah."

"You know how I know that? Because someone is following you and getting real time pictures. One just got posted of you on the corner by where the electric cars charge, and you're on your phone. You're wearing your Seahawks sweatshirt."

I looked down at my Hawks sweatshirt then over at the charging stations. Chills ran down my arms. With my head on a swivel, I took in the parking lot, looking for anybody, someone ducking low in a car, or someone pretending to be a shopper. Not seeing anything, I fast-walked to LC and got in, hiding behind his tinted windows, afraid that whoever was taking pictures of me was also standing by listening.

In a quiet voice I said, "I sent you photos of a security camera. I need to know the night capabilities. I just came from talking to Caleb. He mentioned someone following and watching him. Called him The Shadow Man. I'm not sure if this person exists. I tried to get the videos from the store's cameras, but I'll have to wait for the manager."

"Sam, in the game *Shadowland Walker,* there is a character called The Shadow Man. He's an omen of bad things to come. He's an NPC, a non-player character, but he's got some type of wicked coding because he's one of the scariest characters in the game."

Learning this made me once again question Caleb's grip on reality. "Send me the links of what you're seeing online." If I were being watched right now, then I'd like to find that person.

"I don't think that's a good idea," Toby said. "We can look at it later tonight, but I think you need to keep your head in the game. Watch your six. Maybe get out of there."

"Toby, send me the link of what you're seeing online. Maybe I can get an idea of where the person took the picture from. And if I can figure that out maybe I'll find some other information."

"That's what I was afraid of," he mumbled. My phone chimed a second later with a text. It was the link.

"Then find out about those cameras. And dig more into Addie Milner. Caleb said she wanted to live with Lora and Nessa, but they'd never invited her to move in. Maybe she's got a chip on her shoulder from being excluded. She's not listed as a member of the team, per se. She doesn't get credit for any of the online stuff. She's support staff. Maybe she's jealous."

"Will do, boss. What do I do about you-know-who here, still chewing her nails and pacing?"

"Let her. This is a process for her. If she starts eating your snacks, call me back. Because that's the real tell."

I clicked the link and played my fingers along LC's steering wheel while I waited for the site to load. The number of pictures was slowing the site's load time. I took the opportunity to survey the parking lot again. I just couldn't see anyone. They were a ghost. They were good. Spooky good. Were they part of the hit? Or Nessa's case? I hated not knowing. Could it be Caleb? I hadn't seen a camera in his apartment, but I hadn't searched it.

My phone chimed with a second text.

TOBY

Start here. www.morningover-
portlandtv.com/gamerdeath

The link took me to the video of Catherine's interview. Near the end was a follow-up link to the show's Facebook page. I dreaded reading that. Social media gave people the sense that they could behave however they wanted because they didn't have to look the person they were dissing in the face. Which meant, people were downright ugly to each other.

The second link Toby had sent was to a Reddit thread.

That couldn't be good. I decided to go with the Facebook page. Again with the replay of Nessa's mom on the talk show. I scrolled to read the comments. Many offered condolences to Catherine for the loss of Nessa. There was also a lot of love for Lora and Nessa.

Then the train jumped the track. Someone named Rob Robbins, clearly a fake name, posted a picture of me at the grocery store, another sitting in my car looking at my phone, and a link to the Reddit thread.

I clicked on the picture, then zoomed in slightly. Based on the angle of the picture, the person had likely been near LC to get this specific shot. That was disturbing, and the hair on the back of my neck lifted. I scanned the cars parked in front of and beside me. Empty.

Had the person been on foot? I clicked on the Reddit thread. More pictures.

Me inside the grocery store talking to Bogey. Thankfully, there was no video or audio of our conversation. Me coming out of the grocery store and looking up at the camera. Again, the angle looked to be coming directly from where I'd parked LC.

Suddenly, I didn't feel like my vehicle was safe. I wanted to sprint from my car, but I also didn't want to play my hand. One thought continued to race through my mind. Had someone tampered with LC?

I blew out a slow, steady breath and tried to calm my nerves. From my messenger bag, I took out a bug sweeper. LC was awesome and old. I didn't bother locking the doors because he wasn't one of those SUVs that got stolen and chopped down for parts. LC required a lot of gas and oil and sometimes smoked like a chimney.

He could be unpredictable. And everything about his presence told people that. So I never felt like he was at risk of being stolen. In hindsight, my naiveté gave another person easy access to my vehicle to do whatever. Like plant a bomb.

With a shaky hand, I began sweeping the interior of my car. Within four seconds, I found the bug. The little sucker had been embedded under my driver's seat. Not the best place for a microphone, but not the worst either. Whoever bugged my car knew I knew about The Shadow Man, as well as Addie's possible motive. One thing I hated about being a PI was that sometimes I felt two steps behind and never one step ahead.

Maybe this was pathetic, but I kinda hoped Carson was out there, watching me. He'd spent the last six months to a year watching my back. I wouldn't mind that today. Pathetic or not, knowing he could be out there made me feel less alone.

I pondered my next move. Do I tip my hand and show the person I found the bug by stepping outside and sweeping my car for anything more? Or do I keep the bug right where it is and hope that when I start the engine my car doesn't explode.

CHAPTER FOURTEEN

START THE CAR OR TIP MY HAND? THIS WAS A MAJOR decision. Something big could happen or nothing at all. Yet, this wasn't a decision I felt like I could make in thirty seconds or less.

I wanted to get out and sweep the car to see if I was, at best, being tracked, at worst set up to go boom. If there was a tracker, I couldn't say for sure it wasn't put there by Carson. I mean, there is a hit out on my life; tracking me made sense.

That's when the answer hit me. I didn't have to do anything right now. If someone other than Carson wanted to track me, then they'd have to follow me. Instead, I reached into the storage area that I'd had created below the floorboard behind the driver's seat. I pulled out my camera and attached a long-range lens to the end. Yeah, my car looked like junk, but there was gold hidden in its depths.

I surveyed the area. Because at that moment of clarity about the tracker, I also had clarity about the image. All the images were up close, giving the feeling of being nearby, but that didn't mean the person was as close as I first thought. I was a photographer, so I knew how to make pictures look up close. Lenses were amazing tools, and I could do a lot with them and Photoshop. I'd worked in a photography studio where I learned to make families look way better on film than they did in person. And in my experience with photography as a private investigator, I wasn't afraid of using deep-fakes to get some information.

I looked though the viewfinder toward the direction I felt the photos came from, which was across the parking lot, perpendicular to the grocery store. There was a bank and a fast-food joint and a third building under construction. The sun reflected off something shiny and caught my eye. I looked up from the viewfinder toward the area and strained to see what could have made that reflection. I saw nothing. Going back to the view finder, I zoomed in and waited. Seconds later, the surface reappeared. It was another camera. Right there, on the top of the construction building was a man with a camera with a telephoto lens looking right back at me. To get a better, clearer shot I needed to not be looking through the windshield.

I got out of LC and leaned across the hood. I snapped some pictures, then waved. And because I have a mean streak, I also flipped him the bird. I moved my camera over all the cars parked in the fast-food and bank parking lots and started taking pictures of license plates. It was a crapshoot, but maybe the person on the building had a car parked among these.

I deposited my camera on the passenger seat. Now I had to deal with my fear that maybe my car would explode when I turned it on. And knowing there was a contract out on my life, I just couldn't take the chance. I considered texting Precious, thinking maybe she could use the distraction. But being interrupted when trying to work through something was frustrating, not helpful. I texted Leo.

Busy?

LEO

Doing paperwork

I'm at the grocery store by the roundabout.
I could use a ride. I'll explain later.

LEO

On my way.

I leaned against LC, and while waiting for Leo, I decided to read the comments on the Reddit thread. Any and all information was good information, even if it was gonna hurt to read it.

LaceyRN: *What a tragic loss. If Nessa wanted a life coach she should have a life coach. We are all accountable for our choices.*

Chuckypizza: *Yeah. But Nessa wasn't hiring a life coach. She hired a private investigator posing as a life coach. Don't you think it's odd that this life coach "has also been involved in another crime". Does anybody remember AJ Gunn?*

TreetopTimbo: *I'm not sure if this Sam person is the worst PI or the best one. You have to admit big shit happens around her. Austin Strong's in jail. AJ is a franchise quarterback. She's brought down companies and been in explosions. Maybe she's an adrenaline junkie.*

Ican'tdrive55: *An adrenaline junkie to the point that she would kill a client just to get 15 minutes of fame? And she's the one saying that Nessa was murdered. Right? So maybe she is a camera junkie.*

What? How had these people found out I was investigating Nessa's death as a homicide?

I refreshed the page to look for new comments. To my horror a link with a video of Lora had been posted three minutes before Ican'tdrive55's post.

I clicked the link and held my breath. A reporter had caught up with Lora outside her home. Or maybe Lora had been in the backyard and the reporter had hopped the privacy fence. But Lora was walking toward her house "No comment," she repeated to every question.

Until...

"What do you have to say to Catherine Siegel's accusation that hiring a life coach directly impacted what happened to Nessa?"

"I'd say that wasn't true."

"Lora! Lora?" the reporter shouted. "What are you gonna do now that Nessa's gone? What happens to your company?"

Lora stopped and looked directly at the reporter. "There is no company. It took two people to make that company, me and Nessa. Now that Nessa's been murdered, how could I ever move on? How can I ever keep that company going? She was the heart and soul of it."

"Murdered?" the reporter jumped on Lora's remarks. "What do you mean murdered. Who do you think murdered Vanessa? Why do you think she was murdered?"

Lora's eyes went wide, and instead of closing her mouth, she did what everyone does when in her situation. She tried to take back what had come out. "I think my best friend did an excellent job of managing herself. I don't think she was unhappy with life. And I don't think that what happened to her was an accident, because she was too smart and too diligent for that. That leaves only one other explanation."

The reporter shoved a mic closer to Lora. "Is that why you hired a private investigator? Did you know someone was trying to murder Nessa? Why were you telling everybody she was a life coach? What are you hiding? What do we not know?"

Lora's father stepped through the sliding glass door and put his hand up in front of the camera. "No more questions. You are trespassing. Get off my property before I call the police."

Lora's father hustled her back inside the house, closing the door and curtains behind them.

The reporter faced his camera, looking hard into the screen and said, "Vanessa Taylor murdered? What do we say about that?"

Leo arrived in his official cop car, a dark SUV. I grabbed my camera and messenger bag and was in the SUV in seconds.

He was unfastening his seat belt when I jumped in and slammed the door. He looked startled.

"What's going on? What's wrong." He refastened his seat belt.

I turned my back to the construction building, thinking there was no way I was going to give Mr. Camera a chance to read my lips or film me to read my lips later. "Toby found some pics of me online. They're real-time photos. Taken moments ago. And they looked like they came from where I parked LC. I swept my car; it's bugged. And if you'll notice the construction behind me, there's a guy, or at least there was few minutes ago, with a long-range camera snapping shots. I got a few of him myself. He knows I know he's there. I didn't want to start LC in case he's rigged it to explode. I mean, it's stupid to do that in a grocery store parking lot, but in my short time being a PI, I've come across my share of stupid, brilliant, and psychotic. In this world, there are no rules."

Leo nodded once and put the car into drive. "Good call. Let's get out of here and regroup. I can come back later and sweep the vehicle and look underneath."

"I know this doesn't make sense, but I don't want him to see us do that." I did a slight nod toward Mr. Cameraman.

"I'll make sure he's not up there when we do."

I surveyed the shops and restaurants that surrounded the grocery store. Cameras were everywhere. "I need to see if I can get some footage from these businesses. Or see if Toby can hack into their systems."

Leo groaned. "Please don't say that out loud. You remember that I'm a cop, right? Serve and protect *and* uphold the law."

I gave him an apologetic grin. "I did say try to get the footage first if that's any consolation."

"It's not." He winked and pulled away from the grocery store.

I open the viewfinder on my camera and tried to zoom in on Mr. Camera. He'd done a good job of cloaking himself, the camera blocking most of his face. But I could make out that he was white, with dark hair. He wore a ball cap with no logo on it. Nothing. Just a solid blue ball cap.

Next, I scrolled to all the cars and began jotting down the license plate numbers with make and model in the Notes app on my phone. I'm sure there was some software that could scan all the tags as easily as I could write them down, but I was feeling restless and a bit useless and needed a task.

A text from Lora interrupted my work.

LORA DARLING

I'm sorry. I was caught off guard, and I'm sad and angry, and I just…

It's okay. I totally understand.

…

THE THREE LITTLE DOTS DANCED FOR A BEAT. MY PHONE PINGED.

But I outed you online. They're just saying awful things.

Online is where the trolls live. What the people who care the most about me say is all that matters.

I wish I could say the same.

I DICTATED MY NEXT MESSAGE.

It takes time to develop a thick skin. Do yourself a favor and log off. Look away. Find something else to do. If you must know what's being said, have someone else read things and whitewash it for you. Know what I mean?

There was a long pause. Her three dots in the bubble indicating she was typing appeared and then disappeared. Then reappeared. Finally, a message.

That person was Nessa.

My heart broke into a thousand pieces. What would I do without Precious? I couldn't even picture it. I had Hue, and now Leo, but Precious was my person. She knew where I kept the bodies. Heck, she'd helped me hide some of them. Now, knowing that her friendship with me had compromised her business and reputation, it busted me wide open. I've always believed that nothing on this earth could come between us, but maybe I was wrong. Maybe this was it.

I typed

> I'm sorry. There aren't any words that will make you feel better.

> But finding her killer will. I'm counting on you

I was counting on me too. Because if someone killed Precious, I'd not rest until I brought them to justice.

> Nothing will stop me.

Unless I was murdered before I closed the case, of course.

AT MY APARTMENT, Leo followed me inside. I tossed my messenger bag on the couch and almost followed it, exhausted. But I straightened and turned to survey my apartment. My heart thumped, my paranoia on overdrive. If my car had been bugged, what about my house?

"You should text—"

I slapped a hand over his mouth.

"I will." I gestured for him to zip it. Then I removed my hand and went for my bag where my scanner was. "Want any coffee?" Mindless chatter to make it seem like we were ignorant.

I began sweeping my living room, starting with where I was standing.

"I can make it," he said and went into the kitchen. He pointed for me to go into the bedroom when I was done. From my drawer, he took out a second sweeper and started on the kitchen.

Was it good or bad that I had multiple sweepers and had done this before? I was going with good.

His sweeper lit up at the bar that sat between my kitchen and living room, strategically placed in between the rooms to catch all the words. Leo gave me a questioning look.

I moved toward the tiny mic placed in the small lamp, sitting on my counter, and leaned in close.

"Nope, never, not a chance. Game on." I ripped the mic from the lamp. It was wireless which meant it was Bluetooth enabled. Which also meant someone had to be nearby listening unless a recording device had been set somewhere.

I stormed to my front door and ripped it open, hoping to catch someone doing something to tip their hand.

Instead, Toby and my dad stood at my door. My dad's hand was raised as if about to knock.

"Hi." Dad lowered his hand. "We weren't sure you were home, but we heard movement, so we thought we'd come up and see. Where's LC?"

I glanced at Toby and wondered how much he had told Dad. "At the grocery store parking lot. LC was running rough, and I don't have the time right now to take him in. So Leo came and got me."

I stepped aside to let them in.

"We found something you're gonna find interesting," Dad said.

"Aren't you supposed to be resting?" I pointed at the center of his chest.

"From the stress of the paper. This is just internet research. What's stressful about that?" He settled in on the couch. Toby dropped down next to him.

I handed the tiny mic to Leo.

Leo said, "I'm making coffee. Anyone want any?" He placed the mic on the counter and pulled out the large metal can of coffee beans. He smashed the can over the mic, crushing it.

Dad jumped. "Whoa."

"Sorry," Leo said. "Bug on the counter."

Dad shook his head. "I'll make sure to call the pest control company. You shouldn't have bugs on your counter."

Leo and I smiled at each other.

"You should make sure there aren't more in the house," I said.

He nodded. "I'll do that before I start the coffee."

We traded places, and he went off to check my bathroom and bedroom.

"So no takers on the coffee?" I stalled.

Toby gave me a puzzled look. "Don't you want to know what we found?"

I nodded emphatically but kept stalling. "I do. I just need coffee first."

"I can tell you while you make it."

"Or"— I slapped my hands together in fake merriment— "you can show me and see if I can figure it out. Making me work on my sleuthing skills."

"You're acting weird," Toby said. He faced my dad. "She's acting weird, right?"

"It's me. All the women in my life think I'm fragile and

shouldn't hear anything outside of the weather and the clues on Jeopardy. As if I'll have another heart attack at any moment."

"You did scare us, Dad." I held up a finger, then proceeded to grind some beans, taking a tad longer than normal.

Leo came out of my bedroom a moment later and gave me the thumbs up. "I have to step outside for a few minutes. Police business. I'll be back."

I knew he was going to look for someone, like I had been moments ago. Though the moment was probably long gone.

I quickly put the grounds in the machine and set it to brew. Then I walked over and sat in the chair across from the couch and gave them my undivided attention.

"Okay, tell me. And I'll pretend that my dad isn't here and that whatever you tell me isn't stressing him out."

"What we found doesn't stress me out. It's exciting. Show her, Toby," Dad said.

Toby spun his laptop screen so I could see. "We knew there was spyware on Nessa's and Lora's computers. But I finally traced it. A few months back, they both clicked on an image in an email. It was from Addie, and the image was of them at a gaming convention. Caleb is in the picture. Spyware was attached to the image."

"Why would Addie put malware on their computers? Caleb said she wanted to live with them, but they never invited her to do so. Are we looking at a wanna-be-included-type scenario? That she watched them from the solitude of her apartment, building up resentment?"

"Maybe. Lora opened the image from her laptop, Nessa from her desktop. So, for Lora's camera to work, her laptop had to be open, but Nessa's was an open portal for eavesdropping. Lora also had it on her gaming computer. That looks to have been manually installed. And the install date is a few days after they clicked on the image on their other computers."

"Because Lora tried to keep her gaming computer clean, she didn't check email from there. You said Addie sent the image with the spyware. Why not manually install it like she did on the gaming computer?"

"Because getting them to click an image is easier than sneaking around to install software."

I could see his point. "Maybe. But if Addie wanted to watch Lora and Nessa, she'd put little cameras around their place, because they aren't always around their computers. They even mentioned how they liked to take breaks from being online." I let these facts roll around a bit. "I don't like the inconsistency here. Why not on Nessa's laptop, too?" I stood. "I need to go sweep their house again."

"Sit, Sam," Dad said. "There's more."

I plopped back into my chair.

"Russ and I have been going through gaming forums and such. Remember Winnie Dunlap?"

I nodded.

"She been on the attack. A few months back during a competition at the Seattle Gaming Con, Winnie had people flood Lora during the game. Bogged her down and rendered her useless. She'd start a quest, and they'd attack, killing her character and making her restart. Lora never even spent more than two minutes in the competition and had to bail. She was eliminated. And we have several more incidents like this. Plus, some of Winnie's online threats are similar to the emailed threats Lora got."

"Winnie doxed Lora and gave out her home address,

too," Dad said. "Two weeks ago. She gave it to a guy who was threatening Lora and Nessa."

"Oh, and the spyware put on Lora's gaming computer was specific to keystrokes. It's a keylogging software."

"Keylogging?"

Toby's brows went up. "It logs keystrokes, so it could be used to say ... see what moves a person does during a game."

I started reading the thread on Toby's computer. Chills ran down my spine. Winnie Dunlap wasn't keeping her motive or intentions a secret. Now I had two suspects.

CHAPTER SIXTEEN

Leo dropped me off at the grocery store parking lot, and I spent Wednesday morning on top of the construction building looking for a clue as to who Mr. Camera could be. No cigarette butts, not a hair, not even a footprint. It was the cleanest construction site I'd ever seen.

Afterward, I went to every shop asking about cameras, and if they kept their footage. Most places were on a twenty-four-hour loop, where the footage was replaced by the same hour the next day. And since I didn't have anything specific about a shadow man, I couldn't ask for a certain time or day. The grocery store was my best hope. Their camera's placement was perfect. Toby could possibly hack into the grocery store's security cloud. But a few months back, one of the tech gurus who had built the store's security had been thrown in prison for misuse and fraud. So a lot of systems had beefed up their security. Sometimes I did really good work. I mentally patted my back for that one, though right now, it was biting me in the butt. Hitting a bunch of dead ends, I decided Addie needed to be my next stop.

I got coffee and LC, who hadn't had a bomb in him but did have a tracking device, then I drove across the street to the other set of apartments. According to my records, Addie drove a light-blue Honda Fit. Because Lora had shut down all business, I expected Addie to be at home. Nowhere in the parking lot was that car.

I made my way to the third floor and Addie's apartment and knocked on her door. When she didn't answer, I knocked again. When she didn't answer a third time, I loudly said her name hoping to draw out her neighbors. No one was around. Following a quick survey of the stairs, parking lot, and green space surrounding the complex, I took my lock-picking tool from my messenger bag and went to work on Addie's front door. Within minutes I was inside. And there was no alarm set. No deadbolt. Another place with bad security.

I made sure to leave the door ajar, and to keep from leaving any fingerprints, I pulled latex gloves from my back pocket.

Her living room was also her office, and on a small corner desk, a laptop was open with the screensaver on. There was a printer, a charging port, yet very little paperwork. Next to the laptop was a planner. I opened the planner and, being overly cautious, used the eraser end of a pencil to flip through the pages. It was Lora and Nessa's schedule. I used my cell phone to take pictures. I wanted to see if Addie's planner matched up to Nessa's.

When I was done, I left the planner as I found it and went into her bathroom. Nothing in the medicine cabinet other than aspirin, toothpaste, and dental floss. Nothing under the sink either, no surprise vials of Warfarin.

Once I finished in her bathroom, I went to her bedroom.

She had a bookshelf filled with romance novels and pictures. Many of Lora and Addie, Addie with Nessa and Lora. One of Nessa, Addie, Caleb, and Lora at a gaming convention. I took pictures of her pictures, and then because I felt like I was on borrowed time, I made my way out of the apartment, making sure the door was locked behind me. I walked around her floor looking for cameras but came up empty.

I was heading down the stairs when voices traveled upward. I paused. One of the people sounded like Addie, so I waited on the landing until they approached. Sure enough, when they came around the corner, one was Addie. The other, a mousy, brown-haired girl. I recognized her instantly. She was Winnie Dunlap, the competitor.

"You two are an interesting pair," I said.

Addie's mouth fell open. "What are you doing here?"

"I came to talk to you. I'm surprised to see you with Winnie."

Winnie said, "Why are you surprised? Addie is an amazing assistant, and now with Nessa gone, she's looking for a new job."

"But doesn't she have a job with Lora?" Talk about your loyalty.

Addie wrung her hands. "It's over. Lora won't do anything without Nessa."

"Maybe that's true. But don't you think it's a little early to make that assumption?" I studied Winnie. Did she have the constitution to take a life to win a sponsorship from a network?

Addie leaned against the stairwell wall. "Lora has said she's not going to keep the company."

Winnie pointed to Addie. "She knows Nessa was the brains. Lora was just the person who did the gaming."

I pointed a finger at Winnie. "I know about you. I know what you've done to Lora online. How you crossed the line."

She guffawed. "That's just everyday normal online gaming tactics."

I raised my brows. "Really? Because a lot of what you'd done is against the law. Short of swatting someone, you basically behaved like a stalker, and I can present that to a judge."

Addie gasped and covered her mouth. From between her fingers she said, "Oh, my gosh, oh, my gosh, it's true what they say about you online."

"What's that?" I asked.

"You're a private investigator, aren't you?"

From my messenger bag, I pulled out my ID and showed it to them. "Yes, I'm a private investigator."

Addie reared back as if she'd been hit, then began flapping her hands in what looked like nervous energy. Her voice went up several octaves. "Does that mean that they're investigating me? Does that mean that they think I've done something? Why are you looking into me? What is it that you think I've done?" Her anxiety was escalating fast.

I snatched her hand out of the air and held it. "You need to take a deep breath. Right now, the person that keeps popping up on our radar is Winnie here. Though it doesn't look good with the two of you here together, do you want to tell me what this is about?"

Winnie put a hand on Addie's shoulder and stepped closer to me. "I don't have to tell you anything. Nessa is gone. Addie is looking for a new job. I'm looking to up my business, and Addie has experience with that. Now, with Lora likely finished, I'm the next best candidate for the kids' streaming service sponsorship. I gotta get serious about my business. So yeah, maybe this doesn't look good, like I'm trying to poach Addie, but right now, she's the one with all the skill. And I need that skill."

Wow, this gal had no empathy and possibly no remorse.

"You've been talking to Addie a long time? I asked because you seem pretty familiar with each other."

Winnie gave a one shoulder shrug. "Yeah, well, we've been to conferences together. You can't be in the same world and not know each other."

I narrowed my gaze. "Somehow, I don't think that's the whole truth." To Addie I said, "If you're hiding something, I'll find it. I may already have."

Addie promptly burst into tears. "Is it true you and Lora think Nessa was murdered? Because I was there. I didn't see anybody do anything to her."

"No, but you might've been the person who delivered the poisoned food. Tell me where you got the boba tea."

She swiped tears from her cheeks. "From the boba tea place in Camas. It's their favorite. We have a standing order. I go there three times a week."

"And when you opened the mochi box, it was brand new? Or had it already been opened?"

More tears streamed down her face. "I don't know. I wasn't paying attention."

"Whose idea was it to throw all of that out the very next day?" She had said Walt, I wanted to know if her story would change.

"It was Walt. It was because Catherine was coming over. I told you that."

I decided to go hard on Addie to see if I could break her, or to see if Winnie would react. "Either you poisoned Nessa and Lora or you're an accomplice. Which one is it?" It would be awesome if she just came clean with everything. But that only happened in movies and books.

"No, no, no." Addie clutched my arm. "You have to believe me! I didn't do anything except what I always do. I pick up the tea. I ordered the food. I set it out. I ordered the pizza, and I just serve it when they want it. I know the routine. I stuck to the routine."

"But your tea didn't make you sick, did it? And Caleb's didn't make him sick either."

Addie shook her head.

"Did you go to Caleb's every time before you delivered the drinks to Nessa and Lora?"

"Yes, he likes them, too, and Lora and Nessa never minded that Caleb was included."

"When you delivered Caleb's drink, where were all the teas?"

Addie looked confused. "I don't know. I left them in my car. I just took his cup up to his apartment." She used her sleeve to wipe away her tears.

Winnie stood to the side, listening, arms crossed over her chest.

"How long were you there?" I peppered her with questions, giving her little time to think of her response.

"I don't know, minutes?"

"A few minutes or more than a few minutes? Because when you came into the house that night you were rushing and said you were sorry you were running late. What held you up?"

Addie cast her eyes down and sank to sit on one of the stairs. "Maybe I was at Caleb's for like fifteen or twenty minutes."

"And the drinks were in the car the whole time, correct? Was your car locked or not?"

"Yes, my car was locked."

I leaned in close using intimidation. "And Caleb was with you the whole time?"

"Yes, of course."

In a flash, I turned my attention to Winnie. "And then where were you that night?"

Winnie rolled her eyes. "Well duh, I was online. You can verify that I was in my house getting ready for the game. I think there might have even been a video of it on my YouTube channel."

Wasn't that a convenient alibi? I narrowed my eyes. "I will verify it. I'm also going to make sure you weren't using a VPN to throw your location and not using a fake background to make it look like you were at home. That your video isn't a deepfake." I handed both of them my business card. "If there's more you want to say, call me. Because right now, neither one of you look really good. And yes, I do think Nessa was murdered."

CHAPTER SEVENTEEN

BEFORE LEAVING ADDIE'S COMPLEX, I CHECKED MY phone to see if there was any news. People on social media were battling it out, picking sides for or against Lora. Precious had texted to say she was trying really hard to shut it all out, that this was a test of her mindset abilities. Knowing I couldn't do anything about those online, I decided to drive to the boba tea shop in Camas and follow up on Addie's story.

As I was driving out of town, I passed the dog park and noticed Paulie Bea and his dog, Rocket, making a loop around the perimeter of the park. Without thinking, I jerked my steering wheel to the right and pulled into the parking lot. Usually at the park were two ladies who made obnoxious use of a whistle calling out other dog owners any time their dog acted like ...well, a dog. Today it was just Paulie.

I let myself in the gate, pulled my rain cap down over my braid and slogged my way across the sloppy grass and mud to where Paulie and Rocket were walking. Paulie was tossing a ball and Rocket would run after it and bring it back.

Rocket saw me, forgot the ball, and came barreling across the park. I braced myself for the impact from the giant schnauzer. Moments later, I was covered in mud and dog kisses as he jumped all over me.

"Rocket, down," Paulie called as he made his way to us. "You're gonna need to change your clothes."

"Yeah, that's okay." I rubbed Rocket affectionately with both hands. "He's a good boy, and I could use the dog love."

"What's got you down?" Paulie handed me a Milk-Bone to give to Rocket.

"This case is a big deal. It feels like everything is imploding, and the lives of the people around me are falling apart because of this case. All because I got a weird feeling about Nessa's death. No one else believes she was murdered."

"You do. Didn't we all spend half the night working through the possibilities of that? Your facts as to why you think she was murdered sound plausible to me."

I chewed my lower lip.

"You think we're backing you up because we're your friends?" He looked knowingly at me. "That we're just telling you what you want to hear?"

"Not you, but maybe Toby and Precious. And not on purpose. I think they want to believe Nessa was murdered because why put ourselves through all this for nothing?"

"That's valid, but you recognize that, so what is really hanging you up?"

"I want to do more than insurance cases."

"You want to add to your PI chops, I get it."

I stuck my hands in my jeans pockets. "And yet I might have ruined Precious's business in the process of building mine."

He shook his head. "Catherine Siegel is the one doing that."

"I can't be mad at her. She lost her child."

"Sure you can, but I get why you aren't." He gestured for me to spill my guts. "You're holding back. Just say it."

I kicked a small clot of mud, then picked up Rocket's ball and chucked it across the field.

"I'm not doing a good job here, Paulie. Things are on fire all around me, and I can't put a single flame out. I can't even get access to what I need. Like the assistant manager at the grocery store can't even be bothered to look at security footage. I have Toby trying to find a back door, but I'd like to be as legit as possible in this case. I want every piece of evidence to stand and be used."

Rocket trotted back and dropped the ball at my feet. I tossed it again.

"What's this manager like?" Paulie had decades as a PI under his belt.

There was no doubt he'd have a solution to my problem. "He's young and snotty. Told me to get a warrant."

"Do-gooder?" Paulie looked just as a Paulie should look. Dark shaggy brown hair that was graying. His britches had a hard time staying waist level, frequently riding down to show the waist band of his Fruit of the Looms.

"Yeah, said he didn't believe on trampling people's rights. Said he wasn't gonna invade anyone's privacy."

Paulie's brow quirked. "What did he say when you offered him money?"

"I didn't offer him money. I tried to appeal to his sense of right and wrong. That's when he got all preachy with me."

Paulie shook his head as if I hadn't learned a single thing

from him. "Sam, you gotta be willing to let the money flow sometimes. If you're letting money flow out, then information will flow in. Karma or whatever."

"I don't know how to do that. Do I just put some twenties on the counter?" Let's think about this. I've never had to bribe people before. I scratched my neck near my collar, trying to come to terms with the idea.

"You'll get used to it real quick. But track it because it's a business expense. But what is *really* bothering you?"

"I told you. It's knowing how to get what I want. I can take pictures all day long, but that's not helping me get people to give me access to their security cameras."

Paulie shook his head and spit his gum on the ground. "Listen, this job gets easier when you start telling yourself the whole truth. Your clients are going to lie to you. They're gonna hire you under false pretenses. You think you're getting hired by the good party only to find out the shit bag in the divorce is the one who hired you. You're gonna get hired to do jobs that will turn your stomach. Missing kids, men with other families, grifters, cons. It's not taking pictures of babies dressed as cherubs."

"You're not making me feel any better." I knew all this, but putting it out there made it very real.

"You have the spine for this job. I watched you hunt down a murderer who out-gunned you, out-manned you, and out-moneyed you, all because your friend was on the hook for a murder he didn't commit. You got moxie."

"I hear a *but* coming."

"But what you're not facing is that your job as a PI will bloom regardless of what happens with this case. You're either right or wrong about this girl's murder, but at least everyone will know the truth, and there is peace in that. The hardest problem you're going to have is weeding out the bad gigs. What's bugging you is that your tall and blonde bombshell of a friend isn't going to be so lucky."

My shoulders slumped. "I can't have that."

"Then do something to stop it. Your inaction and lack of response is just feeding the flames online. Talk to your client. Tell her that you're going on the attack or walking away." From his jacket pocket he took out a pack of gum, slid two pieces from the pack and unwrapped them. He tossed the wrappers on the ground and shoved the pieces in his mouth.

I stooped to pick up the wrappers. "Walk away from this job even when I think someone murdered Nessa? Walk away from that?"

"That's what I meant about telling yourself the truth. What means more to you? This job or your friend?"

"Precious, of course." That question was a no-brainer.

He didn't say anything, just stared at me. And I knew. I knew without him having to say the words that my actions weren't saying that I would pick Precious over my job. If anything, my actions said I was hedging my bets. Paulie was right, the truth was out there, but there was no explanation which opened the opportunity for random people to create a narrative of half truths and wild ideas. Soon, no matter what we said, the fictional version of my relationship with Lora and Nessa would be what people thought was the truth. And then there would be no chance of course correction.

"Crap," I said.

"Yeah," he said.

"Woof," Rocket said a second after he dropped his ball at my feet and I didn't immediately pick it up.

I scooped up the ball and chucked it far across the field.

"Thanks, Paulie."

"This won't be the first time you'll find yourself in these situations, kid."

I nodded. "But next time, I won't allow my friends to be involved."

Paulie snorted. "Who are you kidding?"

I waved my hand in the air as if I were trying to erase what I said. "I mean I won't use their businesses as a cover. I'll think twice." *Because who was I kidding?* If I were hunting down a bad guy, Precious would either be driving or riding shotgun, and Toby would be in the back seat.

I left the park and drove straight to Lora's. I told her my plan. I didn't ask for permission because leaving Precious hanging out to dry wasn't an option.

"We can terminate our contract right now. If you want. You can hire someone else to work on Nessa's case and I will be more than helpful with them. But I can't let Precious's business come under fire like this."

We were sitting on chairs on her parents' porch. She tucked her feet under her.

"Nessa is gone. I know she didn't want to hurt her mom's feelings by going behind her back, and I want to respect that. But Nessa was my best friend. She meant everything to me. And if the shoe were on the other foot, I'd do exactly what you plan to do to save Nessa's company. So do it. And no, I don't want to terminate our contract. In fact, I more than ever want to bring justice for my friend."

My heart leapt; this felt like action. Not reaction. Lora and I were in a similar situation, only I knew my friend was at risk and there was a chance I could save her. "You sure? It will probably get ugly."

"It already is ugly." She wiped a tear from her cheek.

I nodded in agreement.

Lora stood. "Here, let me hold the phone while you film your video."

CHAPTER EIGHTEEN

I LINKED MY VIDEO TO EVERY SINGLE POST REGARDING Nessa's death, hitting hard the ones that focused on the role Precious and I played.

In my video, I stood against a stone column that lined the Darling's porch. I told the world my name and my profession. I held up my ID and gave my license number. Anyone could look up my PI information without it; the information was public record anyway. But I wasn't holding anything back.

Then I told the world why Lora and Nessa hired me and how they asked to keep my business with them under wraps. That I knew they were already working with a PI but were uncomfortable with the direction he was going with their case. That Nessa wasn't using a life coach. That Nessa was organized and focused and had mapped out her life goals for the next five years. I showed the camera the image of a Post-It Nessa had put under her calendar. The last line so poignant.

I read it for the audience. "Nessa wrote, 'Reassess after

these five years because I can't begin to imagine how amazing life will be, and I'm so excited to see what the years bring'."

I took the image away and stared into Lora's phone. "These are not the words of a woman who needed a life coach because she was disorganized and scattered. These are not the words of a woman who is unhappy and contemplating the unimaginable. These are the words of a woman who died too soon. Whose desire to see what the next five years were going to bring were taken away from her. And I intend to find out why and by whom."

I swallowed before continuing. "Erika Shurmann of Limitless Life was kind enough to allow me to use her business as a cover to appease Lora and Nessa's wishes to not confront Catherine Seigel. The only fault of Limitless Life is their misfortune of being associated with me. Erika Shurmann and I have been best friends since elementary school. Much like Lora and Nessa. If you understand true friendship, then you'll understand why I am pursing the unexpected death of Nessa Taylor as a murder. If you have any information, you can email me at STrue@Trueinvestigations.com"

Lora spun the phone around so she was looking at the camera. "Please," she said. "Please. Do this for my friend Nessa. If you know of anyone who might have wanted to hurt me or hurt her, please let Sam know."

She ended the video and met my gaze. "This is the right thing to do. I can feel it," she said.

I nodded. "We're gonna get the answers, Lora."

She tapped on her phone. "I know. That won't bring her back, but it's better than nothing."

I left Lora to hang with her brothers, and while sitting in

LC, I posted the video. Within minutes, there were comments on the post. My inbox started chiming with emails.

I called Toby.

"Dudette," he said. "It's a hailstorm now. Least you could have done was given me a heads up, and I would have made a new email for you. This one is gonna be useless."

"So you saw the video?"

"Yeah, it's good. Online chatter is starting to shift for the positive for Precious. Many people are understanding about Catherine's remarks. She was only dealing with a portion of the facts when she accused Precious and you."

I let out the breath I'd been holding. "And the focus is on me?"

"Oh boy, is it. Many of your cases are being brought up. You're not-so-real marriage to Carson is all the chat. You and Lora are trending."

"Is that good or bad?"

"We'll know soon enough."

"I need you to get into my work email and start sorting out the emails coming in. I want those related to this case to be in their own folder. I'll go through it and weed out what people are saying."

"How about I get rid of the BS ones?"

"No, I'll do it. I want to see everything."

"It's gonna be hard, Sam."

"Yeah, I know. But that's the job."

"In other news, I traced the IP of the spyware to a VPN. But that's a dead end because it's not like I can find out who has that account."

"I'm guessing to get that legally, we'd need a warrant,

and to get a warrant we'd need a reason with evidence, and we'd have to be the cops."

"Yep."

"But is there a way to get it that maybe isn't fully on the up and up?" I hated to ask. But I wasn't a cop. And weirdly, I saw lines between right and wrong differently now.

"Yeah, it's called scripting, but we need to be right outside the person's house to do this."

"Okay, do you have what you need to do this?"

"Aw, crapola Sam. You sure about this?" The rustling of what was likely a chip bag mixed with his words.

"Right at this moment, yes. Ask me again later. Wait! Maybe don't ask me again. I'll pick you up at half past seven. Wear dark clothes."

"May the Force be with us," he said, strained.

"Oh, don't be such a scaredy-cat. Don't forget you've been shot before, and you came out just fine."

"Tell that to my therapist."

I laughed and disconnected. Toby might protest a lot, but there was excitement in his voice. He just wasn't going to let himself be identified as a thrill seeker. That would go against the lazy, can't-be-bothered, stoner persona he liked to wear. But Toby was anything but lazy.

Leo was bogged down in paperwork. Carson was who knew where, hopefully getting some leads on my hit man, and Precious... well, there were things we needed to say to each other.

I drove directly to her office. Limitless Life was one corner of the third floor of an office building in downtown Vancouver, overlooking the river.

I took the stairs and checked my pulse as I flung open the door to the offices. Heartbeat still good, a positive since I'd been spending a lot of time sitting around in cars, hospitals, and at home.

Precious's secretary, Johanna, was at the desk on the phone. She gave me the one-moment, raised finger sign.

I gestured to Precious's office, but she shook her head and pointed to the other side where the restrooms were.

I went there instead.

The ladies' room had three stalls. The end one was closed. The room was silent except for barely audible mumbling and a sniff here and there.

"Precious?" I said. It's not like we hadn't been in the same bathroom together a million times.

The room went quiet. "Sam?"

"Yeah. What are you doing in there?" I had a sneaky suspicion she was hiding in the restroom.

"Tapping and manifesting." Her admission was quiet. Tapping is a technique of tapping fingers on the body while talking through fears and anxiety.

"Don't you have an office for that?"

She flung open the stall door. "The phone won't stop ringing, and the emails just keeping coming in. It's too distracting. I want to smash my computer every time it chimes." Her eyes were red from crying.

I leaned against a sink. "I'm sorry you've been dragged into this."

"I know you are. I saw your video. You didn't have to do that for me." She moved to stand next to me, leaning against a different sink.

"Yeah, I did. You're more than my best friend. You're family. And this could have come between us. I want to figure out what happened to Nessa, but not at any cost. Lora will never have her best friend again. She will grieve her the rest of her life. I don't want to do the same."

Precious ducked her head. "I know. I could feel this between us. I couldn't be mad because I was on board, but the online hate and canceling is real and scary, and even though I thought I was in a place to not care about that, I realize that I've built a business dependent on what my online presence says about me, and you know what? You know who hasn't canceled me? People who came to me through word of mouth from other clients. Like the two I got from AJ. They've held fast."

"Have you lost a lot of clients?"

"About half. And at first I was freaked out about it. I paid Toby to look online and see what, if anything, they were saying."

"Were they?"

She nodded. "You can learn a lot about people about how they respond to drama or crisis. And some just share everything online. It's very revealing." She brushed a hand through her hair. "From now on, I'm going to sweep people's social media before I accept them as clients. People can be so ugly online. They say things they'd never say to your face."

"Totally. People should be ashamed of themselves."

"Well, you find out quick who your friends are." She placed her hand on my arm and gave a gentle squeeze. "Even Lora has been a better friend than some. It was very brave of her to tell others they hired a PI. That can't be sitting well with Catherine."

"Nessa's mom isn't being very nice to Lora. She's blaming her too."

"Grief can make people act out of character."

"About your clients—"

"Yeah, about them. You know what I discovered?" She didn't wait for me to respond. "I discovered the weaknesses in my business. I don't think my business will survive this, at least not the model I have in place right now. I mean, it'll limp along for a while, but ultimately, what I've had in the past is gone."

CHAPTER NINETEEN

I picked Toby up after sundown. He was dressed in all black and carried two computer bags.

"Why do you have grease marks under your eyes? We doing a flag football game later?" I asked.

"Ha, ha." He held out a can of black face paint. "You want some, because you're as pasty white as me, and I figured for what we're doing, I needed to blend into the night."

"No, because if say, the cops do come upon us, I won't look like I'm doing something wrong." I unzipped my dark-blue hoodie and flashed my white T-shirt underneath. "You, on the other hand look suspicious."

He narrowed his eyes at me. "Are you just saying that to mess with me?"

"A little." I smiled. "Relax. It's going to be fine. Caleb lives on the top floor of the building in an end unit. There's a dark alcove you can tuck into and try your magic. If it doesn't work, we leave, and I'll buy us pizza."

Toby's face split into a grin. "Deal."

The ride to Caleb's was quick. I parked around the back which was poorly lit and occluded by trees. Toby followed me up the back stairs and around to the front to Caleb's. The way the apartments were laid out, there was a small window next to the front door that looked into his foyer.

The outdoor hallway ended, but if I leaned over the railing to look around the corner, I'd look right into Caleb's balcony and his living room and gaming station behind the glass slider.

I signaled to Toby to set up as I took my post as lookout. He had one goal. See if Caleb was using that VPN address and if there was anything on his computer that could implicate him. And if there was, I might have just shot myself in the foot because none of it would be admissible. Once we did Caleb's, then I wanted to try Winnie and Addie, but I hadn't told Toby that.

I stood a few doors down, in a pocket of darkness. From my spot, I could see the stairs and out into the parking lot.

"How's it going?" I whispered to Toby. No one was out, as it had just stopped raining. My whisper the only sound.

"Fine," he whispered back.

"Are you in yet?"

Toby grunted. "Listen, it's not like on TV. These things aren't like plugging in and snapping my fingers. So give me some space will ya?"

"Jeez," I mumbled. "I was just asking."

Toby responded by tapping some keys. I pressed against the wall and surveyed the area.

From the corner of my eye, I caught a spider run down the wall beside me. He stopped, and I imagined him staring at me. Slowly, I turned to face him. He was the size of a quarter. Giant by all accounts, at least to me.

I took a step away. The spider swiveled and ran off, scurrying up the wall and in Toby's direction.

"Psst, I hope you hurry because there's a big, honking spider headed your way," I whispered with force.

"Great, just what I need. More pressure."

"I'm not pressuring you. I've been waiting here quietly for minutes now."

"Yeah, like two minutes. An e-tern-ity." He emphasized the last word, his voice heavy with sarcasm.

I smiled and looked out at the parking lot. This scripting was far easier for me than a stakeout. At least my part was. That's when I saw it. A tiny orange glow in a blob of darkness. A second later, the orange glow flared, shining brightly before fading back to its original color.

Had it not been for the spider, I wouldn't have seen it. I realized, then, the spot I'd been in a moment earlier had directly blocked my line of sight to the strange orange glow.

The Shadow Man?

The orange glow didn't move. Like the person was leaning against the building, which just so happened to be the construction building where I suspected Mr. Camera had been housed. The orange glow was unlikely a worker who stepped outside for a smoke break, the hour was too late for a worker to still be on-site.

Nope, this person was doing what I was doing, using the shadows to observe. What I didn't know was if they were watching me and Toby, or Caleb? What were the odds they were watching someone else?

I tugged my black cap down over my ear, tucking my light hair inside. When I stepped out of the shadows, I wanted to delay drawing attention to my presence.

I slunk down and penguin-walked to Toby.

"Hey," I whispered. This time using the softest whisper I had.

He spun to me, his finger over his lips, his laptop clutched to his chest.

He pointed, curving his finger in the direction around the corner.

Someone around the corner coughed.

Caleb. He'd come out to his balcony.

"I see you," Caleb said.

Toby and I pressed ourselves against the wall, and I stared at the corner. Looking for his face. Had he come out the front door, he'd most certainly have seen us, if not sense our presence, but I couldn't see him leaning over his balcony to look around the corner at us.

I eased up slightly, my thighs screaming in protest as I pressed down on them so I could peek over the side of the exterior wall.

The orange dot was still there.

"You don't scare me," Caleb's voice wavered, indicating his words weren't true.

I sank back down on my haunches and leaned toward Toby. In his ear I whispered what I was going to do, and then I passed him the keys to LC. If he couldn't get into Caleb's internet within the next few minutes, he was to abort and exit back the way we came, trying to stay low and out of sight.

He shook his head in protest, but I ignored him. I hustled back the way I came, staying low.

When I got to the bottom floor, I circled around to the front, using cars as my cover. The construction site was up ahead at my eleven o'clock. I headed to my two o'clock. I wanted to come from the side of the building, but his position was so darn near perfect that there really wasn't a way to sneak up on him unless I left the parking lot entirely and came around from the other side of the grocery store.

There was an open span of parking lot that separated me from who I thought was The Shadow Man, and once I reached the last car for cover, I lay on the ground and mapped out my plan. I had enough shadow that if I moved swiftly, I hoped to make it across the road to where the man was before being spotted. Particularly if his focus was on Caleb.

But before I could launch myself, the orange glow dropped to the ground, a few sparks burst out as if he was snubbing the cigarette out. A car turned into the grocery store parking lot, and the reflection from the lights caught on something where I was staring. A glint, a flash of metal? A watch? Gun? But whatever it was, the man was on the move, and in the opposite direction of me.

This was it. My one chance.

I vaulted from the ground and dashed in his direction. From my hip pocket, I took out a flashlight and pointed the beam in his direction. I was right. He was hustling off. Based on the person's frame, The Shadow Man was indeed a man; he was tall and quick. He had a ski cap pulled low like I did and was dressed in all black.

"Hey! Stop." I yelled, like I was the police or something. I used the same stern voice I used with my niece, Cora, and it worked with her.

Not so much here. This only made the man move faster. His clothes were black and bulky, like sweats, so I couldn't tell if he was lean or not. But once I'd called out, he broke out into a full run. Moving in the direction of the field behind the construction site, away from the grocery store and the apartments. My spidey-sense tingled.

"Behind you, Sam!" Toby's voice rang across the open area.

I glanced over my shoulder and saw another man running toward me. He was also dressed in black and was moving fast, faster than me. He would be on me in seconds.

I turned back toward who I thought was The Shadow Man. He'd stopped and was facing me, his hands out in front. He was pointing a gun in my direction. Before I could pivot or think of anything else to do, like put my hands up or regret my life choices, a solid mass slammed into me from behind, and I flew toward the ground, coming to a stop after a brief slide on the rocky dirt.

A shot rang out.

The person who tackled me, lifted up slightly, the silver metal of his gun gleaming in the moonlight.

I covered my head with my hands and arms and tried to curl up into a fetal position. Hoping if I was about to get peppered with bullets, somehow my position would work to my benefit.

My attacker pulled the trigger.

Several times.

At The Shadow Man. The two exchanged fire.

Dirt clots flew up around me as bullets sprayed the area.

A sudden burning sensation ripped through my shoulder, and instantly, I knew I'd been shot. But I balled up tighter.

The guy covering me grunted, "Oomph," and slumped over me.

"Dammit, I'm hit," he said.

I eased my hands from my face.

"Carson?"

"Yeah, you hurt?"

I tried to straighten.

"No, don't move." He dropped a clip from his gun and pushed in a fresh one. His breathing was becoming more labored.

"Oh my God, were you hit?" The dark night and his matching clothing made it hard for me to see anything.

The wail of sirens rang out in the distance.

Carson slumped farther, no longer fully covering me. I looked over his shoulder and saw the man running off.

Carson was aiming his gun but his hand wobbled. "If he would just hold still," he grunted.

I unrolled myself and moved to where I could get a better look at everything. The Shadow Man was gone. Now cloaked by the copse of trees that hadn't been razed when they built the new grocery store and adjacent plazas.

We were sitting ducks out here in the field.

"We have to move," I said.

Carson rolled onto his back. "I don't think I can."

He handed me his gun then pressed a hand to his side. When he pulled his hand away it looked wet. Blood.

"What are you doing out here?" I asked him as I tugged off my hoodie and balled it up. I used the flashlight to guide me. Pulling up his shirt I searched his torso for the entry point. To the right of his stomach, I found it. Blood pumped in rhythm with his heartbeat. I pressed my hoodie to the wound. He groaned.

"Jeez now you're even more a target in that white T-shirt."

"Shut up. Focus on not bleeding."

He snorted, then moaned.

"You know you could have been chasing your own contract killer into the woods. Did you ever think of that?"

I hadn't. But I didn't think the guy was there for me. This had been the guy Caleb had mentioned was watching him.

"I said shut up."

But when I looked at Carson to show him I was teasing, there was no point. He'd passed out.

CHAPTER TWENTY

Leo burst into my hospital room while the doc was stitching up my shoulder.

"Hey," I said. "You didn't see my parents, right?"

He was dressed in his detective uniform: dark trousers and a polo shirt with his badge clipped to his belt. "Nope. So far, your secret hasn't gotten out."

"Could you make sure to tell Toby not to say anything? He seemed genuinely freaked out. He was stroking his chest even though Lady M wasn't with him."

"Toby's in the waiting room. I took his phone away. He knows not to say anything. I checked on Carson." Leo came to stand by the bed and watched the doctor with her even stitching. "Wow, you've got seven so far."

"Merely a flesh wound." I used my best British accent. "How's Carson doing? He must have lost a lot of blood because he passed out."

Leo grinned. "I'm sorry I missed that. I think he just passed out from the pain. He's going to need a little bit more work than you, but he's fine. The bullet missed all his major organs. Wanna tell me what happened?"

Even though I didn't have romantic feelings for Carson anymore, he did just take a bullet for me, and was working to keep me alive. A girl had to appreciate that, and I did. I was relieved he was going to be okay. "Well, there are some parts I don't want to tell you about at all, and it would be to your benefit not to know."

"I don't like the way this is starting."

"I wasn't in danger or anything. Toby and I were just staking something out."

"You said staking something out, not someone." He gave me his cop look, the one that could burn holes through walls.

I tried to shrug.

"Hey," my doctor said. "Sit still." Her tone was terse, but her smile was kind.

"I have an issue with VPNs. You really want to know about that, or can I skip to the important parts?" I didn't wait for him to decide. "So there I was, just hanging out at this apartment building when I happened to see this guy, or someone in the shadows, smoking a cigarette."

"How do you stake out a thing?"

"Not really stake out, more like peek inside its closets."

"That sounds like an illegal search." He crossed his arms.

"Toby and I never entered anyone's house or place of business or anything."

He narrowed his eyes like he was trying to work out what I'd been up to.

"Listen, you're gonna have to move off this. Let's talk about the guy with the gun who shot me. Caleb calls him The Shadow Man."

"Oh, like the bad guy in that game Shadow Walker," my doc chimed in.

"You know it?"

She tied off the last stitch. "My son plays it. He loves those two YouTubers. So sad what happened to one of them. My son says The Shadow Man got her. Kids these days, they can't separate game life from real life."

Leo cleared his throat. "Back to this person. Are you sure it was a guy?"

"Not a hundred percent, but my gut tells me it was a guy. Maybe by the way he ran."

He gestured for me to continue with my story. The doc was taking her time, slowly bandaging my arm, clearly interested.

"I decided to try to see who this mysterious cigarette smoker was. I mean it was weird that he was just standing there watching."

"Watching you?"

"I think watching Caleb, but maybe he knew I was there because when I tried to sneak up on him, he took off. I don't know if something or someone spooked him or if he saw me coming."

Leo sighed wearily. He ran a hand down his face. "Please don't tell me you ran after him."

"Okay," I said, giving both him and my doctor a fake smile.

Silence hung between us.

The doctor chuckled. "I think this means she ran after him."

"She always does," he mumbled.

I played with my hair, wrapping a small portion around my finger. It was important that Leo see I wasn't shaken up. That this was all in a day's work. "Should I keep going?"

He gestured irritably.

"There I was, chasing this person, and they were running away from me. Toby yelled that someone was running behind me. Next thing I know, I'm tackled to the ground, and it's Carson. He's shooting at the person I was running after, and that person is shooting back, and I think what happened was a bullet struck the ground and a rock did this to me."

"Girl..." the doctor snort-laughed. "If that helps you sleep at night, then just go with that story."

Leo had come to stand next to my bed, so close I could feel the tension ripple off him. "Let me get this straight. Carson shot at this person, and this person returned fire."

"Yep." I wasn't sure what specifically he had an issue with. In his defense, there were a lot of points in this story that were troublesome.

"And you were only shielded by Carson's body?"

"Yep."

"And you walk away with a graze on your shoulder, and he has a bullet in his right side."

"Sounds like you really have the story down."

Leo shook his head. "I don't know if you're lucky or unlucky."

"Gotta go with lucky," I said.

The doctor nodded in agreement.

His gaze was stuck on the bandage on my shoulder. "And now that you're all stitched you're gonna want to go back out to the site and look around, aren't you?"

I grinned. "Of course, though before I go, I have to double-check some things with Toby."

"How are you going to hide a bandage on your shoulder from your dad?"

"I'm going to wear long sleeves and hoodies; it's cold outside so this is gonna be easy."

"And you're not gonna let him hug you?" Leo gave me a pointed look.

I did come from a family of huggers.

"Maybe I'll fake a cold for a few days."

"Or three weeks," said the doc. "Because that's when the stitches should be dissolved."

Leo asked the doctor, "You think she'll be out of here soon?"

"In a rush to spring me?" I winked at him.

"I figured I'd take you back to the site since that's likely where you're going as soon as they let you go here."

I nodded, pleased that he knew me so well. "I'll want to pop in on Carson first. He did take a bullet for me, after all."

The doctor finished typing in her computer, and seconds later, a printer spit out some papers. "You're officially discharged. Good luck. Though I have a feeling I'll be seeing you again, soon." She winked at me, then patted Leo on the arm before she exited.

"Do you know her?" Leo asked.

I flipped my legs over the bed and moved to stand up. "No, doesn't really bode well, does it, if the doctor is expecting me back soon."

Leo chuckled, holding out a hand to offer support. "Maybe she's just pragmatic."

I let him pull me into a light hug. "Or psychic. C'mon, let's go see Carson."

We found Carson on a different floor under a name I'd

never heard before. He was sitting up in bed eating lime Jell-O.

"This is all they'll give me for now. Can you believe this place? I've had worse gunshot wounds and ate a steak afterward. Jell-O? What a joke." He finished the first container and immediately went for a second. Or from the looks of his trash can, a fourth.

"Yeah, yeah, you're a real man. Bullets and steaks, big deal. What happened out there?" I sat on the edge of his bed, pushing his feet to the side. He winced when he adjusted, and for a brief second, I felt bad. But then it passed.

"I had a lead on who took the contract, and I was trying to run it down." He kept shoveling in the individual cups of gelatin.

"And?" I asked. "What was the lead?"

"Can't tell you."

"Why not? It's a contract on *my* life."

"Because you'll go banging around and messing things up."

I stood and gasped. "Mess things up?"

"Just focus on the case you have, and I'll focus on this." He tossed the plastic container and spoon in the trash.

"You know being dismissive is just going to make her dig in harder, right?' Leo said. He'd stayed by the door and was casually leaning against it.

Carson tossed up his hands. "Fine. My lead said the manager of that construction site is the guy in charge. He knows. I was snooping around there when I saw you being stupid."

I punched him in the arm. "I wasn't being stupid."

"He had a gun. Did you? Any chance you considered that?"

"He might not have fired at me had you not come along. Any chance you considered that?"

He rolled his eyes. "Just stay away from the construction site. I'll take care of that. Can you give me that?"

I shrugged. "A guy watched me from that site the other day. Taking pictures and everything. I got a few questions of my own. So maybe you doing your thing and me doing mine isn't the best idea. Seems our things are crossing over."

He eased back against his pillows and faked a yawn. "Fine, we can do weekly check-ins. And I'll want to see those pictures."

"Yeah, and I'll want to know the guy's name and have Toby do a background check."

"He's already on it. Getting sleepy now. Must be the pain meds kicking in. Come back and get me when I get discharged, please." He yawned a second time and fidgeted against the pillows. "Can you help me fluff these? It hurts when I turn my body."

I snatched a pillow from behind him and held it like I was going to smother him. "You sure you want my help?"

He grabbed the pillow from me. "You're a cruel woman Samantha True. But I'm crazy about you."

"Go pound sand," I said, but smiled. I wasn't crazy about him, but I was once married to him. Sorta. And I did kinda like the guy, not romantically, of course, but I didn't want him dead or as an enemy or anything.

He put the pillow behind his head and settled back in. "And here I took a bullet for you."

"And she's in this position because of you," Leo said, then pushed me out the door.

"He can be so annoying," I said.

"I'm guessing he feels the same about you." Leo ushered

me to his police cruiser. "Toby went home, by the way. He said to call him when you get home."

"I think it's about time I annoy another guy. Let's go to the grocery store. I think there's a security video I want to see."

CHAPTER TWENTY-ONE

AT THE ENTRANCE TO THE GROCERY STORE I PAUSED. "I need you to not go in with me," I told Leo.

"Why?"

"I need to do this on my own. If the kid I tangled with the first time I asked is working and he sees you with me, then he might be more accommodating. I need to do this on my own."

He nodded once in understanding. "And if he's not working?"

"I'll feel that person out, and I'll text you if I need you."

My hoodie was long gone, having used it on Carson's wound. My dark jeans were dirty, and there was a clear tear in my white T-shirt which was ringed with blood. The store knew about a shooting happening outside in the field across from their business. On the ride over, Leo had called the station to see if there were any corroborating reports. People had called in shots being fired. Funny though, as Carson and I had waited for the ambulance, no one other than Toby had approached us. It wasn't until paramedics were on the scene that people came closer.

I was hoping all this was going to work to my benefit.

"I'll grab some steaks and stuff for dinner. If you're up for me hanging out tonight."

"I'm always up for it." I smiled.

We entered the store and bumped fists before parting ways. I made a beeline to the customer-service desk. A teenaged girl was behind the counter tapping pointy nails against the keyboard.

"Hey," I said when she continued to bang the board and not even look up at me. "Is the manager here?"

"He's at the district office. But the assistant manager is in." Still no eye contact.

"Can I see that person, please?" Not that she would even care if I said please.

She stopped tapping and leaned over to a microphone, then clicked a button. A quick humming rang through the store but dissipated as fast as it started.

"Bogey, you're wanted up front." She clicked off the button and went back to typing.

Okay, then. I turned to wait for Bogey. Partly excited to face him again, partly dreading it.

He came up an aisle, moving at the speed of a sloth, his feet slapping against the linoleum.

"Look, Sadie, I told you to be more formal than that when you use the mic. Make it professional."

Sadie with the nails stopped typing, leaned back over the mic, flipped the on switch and said, her mouth close to the mic. "Mr. Winky, you're wanted up front." She clicked off the mic. "Like that?" she asked him, clearly annoyed.

"I told you not to use my last name." He banged through

the mini door that separated the world behind the desk from the patrons in front.

"Whatever, Mr. Winky." She shoved some papers at him. "I put your numbers in. You're welcome." She picked up her purse. "I'll be leaving now like we agreed." And Sadie with the nails was gone.

Bogey Winky turned to face me, and his mouth dropped. "I remember you."

Using every ounce of restraint I had, I refrained from commenting on his name. "I was also one of the people that got shot out there today." I pointed in the direction of the store, then to my shoulder, sticking my finger in the hole in my shirt created by the bullet.

"Seriously?"

"You could check the video footage if you don't believe me."

He narrowed his eyes. "You'd like me to do that, wouldn't you?"

"Yes." I slapped a twenty on the counter. This was a guy who bargained with an employee to do his work. His protest the other day was only talk, straight-up BS.

One brow shot up as he stared at the twenty. "Don't you want more than one date?"

I slapped another twenty and wondered if I could get him to sign a receipt saying he took the money in exchange for the footage so I could put it on my expense form.

"What was that date?"

I slapped another twenty down. "Just give me all of last week and this week if you have it."

He held out his hand.

I pointed to the money.

He pointed over my shoulder. "You'll need a thumb drive. Aisle four, school supplies."

We both lunged for the money at the same time. I got it first. "You get this when I get the videos."

I tucked the bills in my front pocket and made my way to the aisle. I passed Leo looking at wine and gave him a thumbs-up. I grabbed the drive, paid at the self-checkout and was back at the customer service counter in under five minutes.

Bogey took the money and the drive and disappeared through a door behind him.

I hummed while I waited.

Leo checked out and came to stand next to me. "All that talk of bullets and steak made me want red meat."

I smiled. "I think it was just the bullets part. Always makes me want to drink a beer too."

"Yeah, but I went with wine."

"Good call. Keep us civilized."

Bogey walked out from the back room, took one look at Leo and pivoted to return from where he came.

"Whoa," I said. "Come back here."

"Hey, Bogey," Leo said. "How ya doing?"

Bogey turned, his face red. "I'm good, Coach."

I tilted my head in surprise. "Coach?"

"Yeah, you remember Tupi and I run a flag football team, right?"

I nodded. I'd kinda forgotten.

"Bogey used to be on it. Dropped out to pick up more college classes. How are those going?"

"Good, good. I'm almost done with my bachelor's and a year early." His chest puffed out with pride.

"I'm very proud of you for sticking with it." Leo stuck out his hand to shake Bogey's.

"Thanks, Coach." He pumped Leo's hand.

"And I'm sure when the cops asked you all the questions about the shooting earlier, you were very helpful." He turned to me. "Bogey has a valid distrust of the law and social services. It's something we worked on for a while."

"I wasn't here. I was at dinner. Sadie was here. She said no one in the store heard anything. There was only one person in the parking lot, and she overheard one of the cops say that person didn't hear anything other than what sounded like someone crushing a soda can or something. She thought it was the store doing it."

I knew Carson had a silencer on his gun, but apparently so did The Shadow Man.

"Thanks, Bogey. And if you need anything, reach out. If you can't find me, you can always hit up Samantha here. I'm sure she'll be around for a while." He nudged me to start walking out.

I held up a hand for the thumb drive. "Yeah, for sure. And thanks."

Bogey dropped it in my palm, he wagged his brows. "Had you told me you and Coach were ba—"

I put my finger in his face. "Nope. You are dangerously close to crossing a line."

His mouth flapped like a fish as he struggled for a response.

I flicked his name tag before turning on my heel and catching up to Leo.

We made quick work of getting to my house. I texted Toby on the way and asked him to join us.

"I invited Toby," I told Leo as he stood on my back deck firing up the grill.

"I figured. I got food for him too." He gave me a captivating smile.

"It's like you know me or something." I leaned into him and pressed my body to his. I wrapped one arm around his waist.

"Shoulder hurting, huh?"

"Yep," I said, then kissed him long and deep.

Carson was in the hospital and wouldn't interrupt us. Toby would first get high and spend some time with Lady M before he came over. This was his antidote to stress, and there was no doubt today had stressed him out. And the food and video footage could wait.

Right now, I needed Leo. I'd been very cavalier about being shot, preferring to just pick myself up and dust myself off. But now, at home, I was feeling a tad weepy and thankful.

And I really wanted to show my gratitude to Leo.

"Sweetness," he said, nuzzling my neck. "I'm picking up mixed signals."

"What's mixed about this?" I asked while stepping backward, one hand pulling him with me, the other pulling his shirt from his pants.

CHAPTER TWENTY-TWO

LAST NIGHT WENT BETTER THAN PERFECT. ONE, because I was so relaxed by the time Toby arrived, he was instantly calmed too.

Two, the video showed The Shadow Man. The guy with the orange glowing cigarette stood exactly where I'd seen him for several days. Which answered the question I'd had earlier. He was there for Caleb.

But why?

And three? The day Nessa collapsed and was taken to the hospital, the video showed Caleb rushing out of his apartment clutching his folding bike in his arms.

Toby compared the time stamp on the video to his time stamp of events of that day, and Caleb's exit correlated to minutes after Nessa collapsed and immediately after he called nine-one-one.

"Do you think he knew Lora was at the hospital or going there to meet up with Nessa?" I asked Leo and Toby. "And he took his bike, which means he thought that would be faster than a private driver."

The only way to know would be to ask Caleb.

"He's never had a driver's license," Leo said. "Never been arrested, no juvie record, no complaints about him. His college record is uneventful."

"He's a hermit, lives his life online." Lady M's head poked out of her orange carrier and Toby stroked it. "And he doesn't have an account with any of the private driver companies I work for."

I raised a brow in question. "Ah, by chance are you saying you were able to do the thing that we set out to do earlier tonight?"

Leo covered his ears. "Please don't talk about doing things that might not be above board."

Toby and I did faux grimaces

"Well, then you won't want to hear this. But when my system accidentally connected to Caleb's WIFI, I found spyware on his computers as well. And I found the source. He clicked on a pic of Nessa, Lora, and Addie."

Toby pulled up the picture.

"That's the one in his room. Who sent it?"

"Addie."

I sat back and tried to connect the pieces. "Maybe Addie and Winnie have been working together all along."

"That's not all. There's a second signal coming out of his place."

I gestured for him to continue.

"That's why I was having such a hard time getting in today. I was trying to hack the wrong signal. He has a bug in his place. A camera bug."

"He's being watched in his house, and it's not connected to his computer?"

Toby nodded.

"Could it be a security camera?"

Toby shook his head. "After you left the hospital, I went back and joined it. The camera looks at him while he's on the computer. It also shows the living room and kitchen. The info is being stored on a cloud, and it's not his cloud. I traced it but got blocked by the same VPN that was sending Lora and Nessa the threats."

I PARKED LC at the back of Caleb's building and climbed the stairs, retracing my steps from the night before. At his door, I knocked lightly, hoping he wasn't at his computer.

The door cracked open seconds later, the chain still connected. He peeked through the crack. "What do you want?"

"Can you step outside?" I asked quietly.

His eyes narrowed. "Was that you yesterday getting shot at?"

The thing about talking quietly with people is they tended to lower their voice as well. Caleb was no different.

"Step outside, and we can talk about it." I slouched my shoulders and put my hands in my pockets to appear less threatening.

Caleb didn't budge but continued to stare at me suspiciously.

I leaned in close and whispered, "I think your house is bugged."

His eyes widened. His mouth gaped slightly.

"Don't say anything more. I don't know if they are listening."

He put a finger up, then closed the door.

No telling what was going on behind the door. Maybe he knew his place was bugged, maybe he was in on it all along. Maybe my instincts were wrong, and Caleb wasn't innocent. A minute later, the chain rattled, and the door opened fully.

Caleb stepped out, wearing sweats and a ball cap. He closed the door. "You saw him last night, right? The Shadow Man? You were chasing him."

"I can't identify him. I got video footage from the grocery store and watched it last night, and he is outside your house. A lot."

"I knew there was a shadow man. Do you think he's the one who's bugging my house?"

"I don't know, and I don't know where your bug is actually. I just know your house is bugged with a camera, and your computer has spyware. I don't know if there is a mic. I was hoping you'd let me walk around and look."

"Who do you think did this? If not The Shadow Man?"

I held up my hand. "Caleb, I don't know yet. But I promise you I'm gonna try to find out. Right now, Nessa's family thinks that you're stalking Lora, but I don't see any proof of that. And I find it really odd that a person who is accused of stalking another person has a house that's bugged."

He paled and nodded slightly.

I continued, "So we're going to go inside. We're gonna have the same conversation we had the other day. I'm gonna sound like I don't believe you, but I'm gonna be walking around looking for the bug, okay? You need to shut your computer down."

I held up my little scanner. "This is a tool that I will use to help me find it. Hopefully, there's only one.

Caleb slouched against the wall and groaned. This must

be hard for an introvert. He opened the door and gestured for me to precede him. I flipped on my detector and stepped into the space. I kept my scanner by my leg because I knew there was a camera. I didn't know if the bug and the spyware were the same, and I couldn't assume that they were. I waited for Caleb to power down his computer. At least I knew one camera was out of commission. Now to see what else he had.

I began sweeping his apartment as subtly as I could. "Tell me again how you know Addie, Nessa, and Lora."

He stammered. "We ... we..."

We made eye contact, and I gestured for him to take a deep breath.

He did this three times then started again. Repeating his story about how he met them at a convention and cleaned up his online act.

I was sweeping his desk when the light on my detector started blinking rapidly and I focused on trying to isolate the bug.

And that's when a small object caught my eye. It was a gaming bobblehead. The person was holding a gaming device, sitting in a recliner, with a screen in front of them.

Lora had a similar one on her desk. So did Nessa.

Caleb's was a boy. The others had girls.

I pointed to the item, but kept moving, looking for more.

"Why did you go to the hospital that night? You called nine-one-one and then immediately left."

"I knew Lora would be a mess, and I wanted to be there for them when they got to the hospital."

"Where did you think Lora was?"

"Nessa told everyone online that she wasn't feeling well.

I didn't really think about where Lora was. I guess I just thought she was at home on the couch or something."

"Then when you got to the hospital?" Caleb lived closer to the hospital than Nessa, and there was the loss of time it took the EMTs to get to Nessa's house. He left his apartment and went directly to the hospital.

"I heard the nurse talking about Lora being there, and I knew. I knew something bad was happening. I knew someone wanted to hurt them. I could feel it, you know, in my body. Know what I mean?"

"Yeah, I do, actually." More than he knew.

I continued to sweep his kitchen, bathroom, and bedroom. Caleb followed me through the space watching the silent detector. In his room, I pointed to the picture of Addie, Lora, and Nessa on his dresser.

I whispered, "Do you remember where you got this?"

"Addie emailed it to me."

We stood close together so we could talk as quietly as possible. "You printed it out and framed it?"

He nodded.

"This image had spyware attached to it. Did you know that?"

He sucked in a breath, clearly stunned. His eyes misted slightly. "No, why would she do that?"

"Any chance you talked to Lora about game plans? Or about anything gaming?"

"Sometimes. Sometimes we'd get online and play together, just her and I, and she'd show me some moves. Try to help me level up."

"Good moves? Power moves?" I knew little about gaming, but I was trying to understand why a person might want to watch that.

"I was the weakest link on the team. I don't know if I would say power moves."

"What about the bobblehead on your desk?"

"Addie also gave that to me." He looked crestfallen.

I nodded once. "I hate to say this, but I think we need to leave it."

Caleb began shaking his head frantically. "Nope, no way. I can't do it. Nope, no way can't do it." He was stuck on repeat.

"Okay, okay, I hear you. But it has to go. Go get me a brown bag or something I can put it in. I'll see if there are some fingerprints. Maybe that'll give us some information."

He nodded and scurried off to the kitchen to do what I asked.

Five minutes later, I was leaving Caleb's with the little bobblehead in a brown bag. I drove directly to Lora's house and let myself in.

I went to Lora's office first to find her bobblehead, but it wasn't on her desk. I went into Nessa's office next, nothing on hers either. Using my sweeper, I went over both offices again but found nothing. I decided to sweep the rest of the house, but it was also clean.

I stood in Lora's office and stared at her desk. Then I pulled out my phone and flipped through pictures I'd taken. Sure enough, there, next to the computer and a coaster, was the bobblehead.

My pictures dated after Addie had cleaned the house.

Who had come back and retrieved them? Addie? And why and why now? Obviously, the bugs would be of no use now that Nessa was gone and Lora wasn't working.

I sent Lora a text asking for screenshots from her keypad

app of the time stamps when someone had entered her house. And I decided it was time to have a conversation with Walt; PI to PI.

CHAPTER TWENTY-THREE

I made my way to Walt's PI firm, which was located not far from Precious's office. His PI suite took up the entire first floor of a downtown building that overlooked the river, and it was glorious. Lots of glass and steel, plush carpeting, employees walking around earning money for him.

This was what Toby meant when he said we should get an office. This is what my mind conjured up. And in the same second, I saw me in this setting running it, making money, killing it. I thought how Precious had this ability to manifest her goals, and believed she was on the precipice of losing it all. How smart was having a business like this? Did it really mean anything?

A front-desk assistant with perfectly manicured nails and a million-dollar smile sat behind a glass-and-chrome table. She asked, "How can I help you?"

"Hi, my name is Samantha True," I told the receptionist. "I'm here to see Walt." I showed her my identification.

"Oh, I was just reading about you." She quickly smiled

as a sort of apology for her Freudian slip. "Let me tell Walt you're here."

She picked up the phone and a pencil, using the eraser end to tap numbers on the phone. "Walt, Samantha True is here to see you." She listened. "Will do." She hung up the phone, then stood. "Follow me, please."

Wow. I was getting direct access to him. This was gonna be great, and by great I meant awful. We walked through a row of cubicles filled with people printing, on the phone or computers, and I wondered how expensive this was. Couldn't they do this from home and save money?

At the end of the hallway were two large oak doors. The receptionist gave a light tap, opened one of the doors, and gestured for me to enter.

Walt was sitting behind a desk, and when I stepped into his office, he stood.

"Samantha."

"I feel like I should apologize for not being up front with you." I walked toward him with my hand extended. "But Lora and Nessa asked me not to, so I'm sure you can understand. It was a direct request from the client."

He shook my hand, gripping hard. I kept eye contact with him and did not even wince slightly.

"Of course," he said, but the slight sneer of his upper lip told me he didn't. "Perhaps they should've come to me first." He gestured for me to take a seat in one of the plush chairs in front of his desk, and then he sat.

"Well." I took a seat. "That's not for me to say, because I'm not a life coach or anything."

"Often," he said, "I try to guide my clients into doing the right thing."

I gave a gallant shrug. "I don't guide. I list out the options and let them make their own decisions. But we're not here to talk about that. I have some information that I think would be beneficial for you to have." I pushed ahead, not giving him a chance to interrupt. "I know that you think Caleb is Lora's stalker, but I actually think you're looking at the wrong person." From my messenger bag, I pulled out some of the stuff we found on Winnie and placed it on his desk.

"Winnie Dunlap has cozied up to Addie, even used her as a proxy to put spyware on their computers, and I think she even bugged the house using one of these." From the envelope, I slid out a picture of the bobblehead.

"Caleb has one. Lora and Nessa each had one, but they're missing. And if Caleb was stalking Lora, why would he bug his own house? I think his house was bugged because he's easy access to Lora. He's on her team, and he could spill some information to Winnie, who was in competition with Lora and Nessa. We think she's used this VPN to spoof and dox Lora."

He flipped through the papers and pictures I'd put on his desk.

"You're saying Winnie is Lora's stalker?" He pointed to the VPN company. "Lots of people use a VPN. And this is the most popular company. We use it here."

I nodded. "I agree. Only Caleb doesn't use that VPN company. His is different. I'm sure if I were to get a warrant for Winnie's house or this company, we'd see the path leads back to her. She has the motive: Lora and Nessa were beating her out of a very lucrative sponsorship. She has the means: she was using Addie as a proxy to send malware and spyware and was listening into their house. And she had the opportunity because Addie was essentially her cover. You could say she had unlimited opportunity."

"And you think this has something to do with Nessa's death?"

I shrugged. "I don't know if it does, and I'm not going to speculate. I'm not going to rule it out though. Winnie Dunlap went to great lengths to destroy Lora. How far, I don't fully know yet."

Walt studied me. "You've been a PI for what now? A year?"

"A little over, yes."

"You've caught some big cases."

"That's a matter of perspective." Caught being the key word here. Fell into a few out of the necessity to survive and protect my friends and family, for sure. And I would do it again every time.

Walt flipped his computer screen so it faced me. "I've done some digging on you. To protect Catherine, you understand. You've made some powerful enemies."

I waited. Wondering what he was getting at. If Walt was worth his credentials, and if his office was any indication of skill set and success, there was a chance he knew about the contract hit out on me. Suddenly, I felt very vulnerable. Only I couldn't pinpoint why. I couldn't be the only PI with a contract hit out on them. Could I? And like Walt said, I'd had some high-profile cases with good results. When dealing with the underbelly of the world, they didn't always play fair or nice.

"Protect Catherine, how?" I wanted to know definitively where he was coming from.

"If her daughter hires a second PI, going behind her mother's back, I have to make sure that the PI hired doesn't have an ulterior motive."

"You mean to say that you wanted to make sure I didn't

con Lora and Nessa into hiring me? I didn't even know them until last week." I instantly shut my mouth. I didn't owe him an explanation.

"But your IT guy did. Toby Wagonknecht I believe is his name. He was once on their squad in a game."

"Months ago." But Walt knew that. And yet, he'd already created a narrative.

"A few scary emails cloaked behind a VPN, some cleverly placed ads for your services, and nothing comes of it. So you amp up the scary emails."

I held up a hand. "You can't be serious. To imply that I fabricated all this to get a job with them, for what? What would be the endgame?"

"Look at the success you're having. You're all over social media." His lips were pressed into thin lines.

"Oh, yes, all the terrible things people have said about me and Precious have been super wonderful."

"No press is bad press. I'm sure you both have elevated your business's online profile."

It took everything I had to not snort out loud with his ridiculous statement. But something told me he was trying to get under my skin. Which made me realize that I had gotten under his. That knowing Lora and Nessa had hired me to prove Caleb was innocent had not settled well with Walt. And here I sat, telling him he was wrong about Caleb and offering him another possible suspect. One he hadn't found.

Double the ego kick.

Not letting the silence settle between us, he continued, "And I have to wonder, knowing the business as I do and knowing people hold grudges, was Nessa caught in the crossfire of a grudge someone had toward you? Had hiring you cost Nessa her life?"

I stood. "Thank you for your time." I said it only because my mother would hate for me to say the real things that were running rampant in my mind. What I wanted to say was ugly and unprofessional, and I would not stoop to his level.

I reached for the papers and photos I'd put on his desk.

He slapped his hand over them, effectively stopping me from taking them. "I'll be keeping these and anything else you have regarding this case."

"I don't think so. I don't work for you. I work for Lora, and I worked for Nessa. I was sharing out of courtesy." I adjusted my messenger bag, my hands itching to snatch up the papers. I reminded myself that I had copies. "I find it curious that you were adamant that Nessa could have harmed herself. And now, you have shifted that to being in line with what I think. Someone harmed Nessa."

He stood as well and looked down at me. "I think it's possible that Nessa was an unintended victim. That's where we differ. And I'm going to track down every lead and thread that will prove that you know that and have taken steps to cover that up."

Either I was being a scapegoat for the grief Catherine was experiencing or something more nefarious was going on here. My gut told me the latter was true. That I was missing something, not seeing the bigger picture. Could it be something as simple as upstaging this man?

Well, if so, then game on. I just couldn't help myself. I had to challenge him. Definitely a flaw in my character.

I said, "I'll be doing the same. Tracking down every lead and thread and proving that not only were you wrong about Caleb, but Nessa as well."

CHAPTER TWENTY-FOUR

I SPENT THE AFTERNOON GOING THROUGH ALL THE photos I'd taken of Lora and Caleb's homes. Something niggled at the back of my mind, and I just couldn't make it come forward.

The bugged bobblehead was in LC. I wasn't sure what to do with it. I didn't like that spyware had been on Lora's and Nessa's computers, but why would a person need spyware and to bug the house? That was overkill.

My phone chimed with an incoming text.

CALEB

I'm kinda freaked out in my own house.

Yeah, I was prepared for my house being bugged, but that didn't mean I wasn't bothered by it.

I swept your place. It's good.

But I can't shake the feeling that someone was in here.

SAMANTHA: DICTATED

You know that Addie gave you the bobblehead, so no one broke in to plant it.

I mean today. If feels like someone was in here TODAY. I walked to the store to get a sandwich, and when I came back the energy was off.

Chances were, with Caleb, it was all in his head. Totally understandable. But I was one for listening to instincts, so I didn't blow him off. He had, after all, gotten a bad feeling at the hospital.

When did you go to the store?

Half an hour ago. I was only out for 20 minutes.

I glanced at my watch and did some quick math. I'd told Walt that Caleb was innocent a little over two hours ago. That gave him plenty of time to get to Caleb's place.

But why? For what? What was I missing? As much as I didn't want to lean on Precious, Toby, or Leo, I really could have used one of them right now to run through some thoughts.

SAMANTHA

Walk around and look at everything. Anything off? I'll come by and sweep your place again.

CALEB

How soon?

I can be there in twenty.

I looked at the pile of photos around me. That's when I saw it. No bobblehead on Nessa's desk. I'd just assumed she'd had one too. But it had only been Lora. And then Lora's was taken? Had Addie thrown it out that day she'd cleaned the house?

The stalker had targeted Lora. The bobblehead had been on Lora's desk. The excessive meds had been in Lora's favorite foods. Toby had said the spyware had been a keylogger spyware.

I wanted to slap myself upside the head. Of course. A keylogger. How else would a person know gaming moves if they couldn't stand right over someone's shoulder to watch them? They could track the keystrokes. Listening in wouldn't do Winnie any good. All Lora and Nessa did was some smack talk with their opponents and join the team chat. Nothing that would tip their hand.

I need to talk with Addie again. She was the center of all this. First, I texted Caleb.

On my way.

Hurry. I'm freaked out. Bad.

I shoved the pictures into a stack and pushed them under my couch, not because they were riddled with evidence, but because I was lazy and in a hurry.

I grabbed my messenger bag and slipped out, setting the house code behind me. I took the stairs two at a time down to the street, and when I came to the street, I nearly collided with my parents.

"Whoa, where's the fire?" Dad said. He steadied me by grabbing my shoulders.

I winced as his fingers bit into the bandage on my arm,

but quickly covered it by stepping back. "Sorry, lost in thought. What are you two doing?"

"We're headed for lunch," Mom said. "To the café. They have a new farm to table menu."

"Salad," Dad said. "All I can eat is salad." His tone did not imply any happiness.

"You like salad," I reminded him.

"Yeah, when it's an option, not when it's the *only* option." He cut his eyes to my mom, letting me know she was nagging him about food.

I clutched my heart. "My chest hurts, yowl," I mocked. "How's that for an option?"

Mom laughed behind her hand.

Dad huffed and crossed his arms. "Now I feel ganged up on."

I hugged him. "It's because we love you. Maybe have some soup with your salad. I'm sure Mom could look away while you indulged in a cup of something creamy and full of fat."

Mom nodded. "A cup, yes, and I would have to look away. Maybe even go to the rest room. Because I do worry."

He put his arm around her shoulder. "I'm feeling broth anyway."

Mom's smile broadened. "Sam, you want to join us?"

I shook my head. "Rain check. Have to go help someone out."

"Okay," Mom said. "Be careful."

"I always am," I said.

They went up the street, and I went toward LC. I'd had to park the large SUV at the end of a row away from my place, more toward the waterfront, in front of a park. To get to him, I had to cut diagonally across the intersection or cross two streets. Being that it was lunch, the traffic was a little heavier than normal, so I opted for the two streets. As I waited for the light to change, a dark sedan with heavily tinted windows rolled slowly by. My spidey-sense tingled. Blacked-out windows of any make and model was trouble. The drive-by shooting I'd been in had involved a dark vehicle with blacked-out windows. When Stella had been kidnapped, also a dark vehicle, blacked-out windows.

The light turned, and I was given the signal to cross. The car, a four-door Mercedes was perpendicular to me, waiting for their light to change. When I stepped onto the road, their engine revved.

My mind said I was being silly, revving the engine meant nothing. My instincts said to abort! Abort!

Curiosity and the don't-back-down-streak in me that made me a PI, told me to play it out. I accepted that something was going to happen. I just didn't know what. Another drive-by shooting seemed unlikely, as they had ample opportunity. And if they thought to run me down, well that was just stupid. I had more than enough space and time to get out of the way. The Mercedes was heavy and would need more seconds to get acceleration than I would need to dive toward safety.

I began my journey across the street. The other side seemed like a mile away. I strolled like I wasn't worried. That I hadn't noticed them. My hand rested on my messenger bag and the stun gun beneath the fabric. As if my stun gun would have any impact here, but touching it gave me comfort.

I was only a few steps into the crosswalk when the engine revved again, and the tires squealed as the car peeled out of its spot.

Holy crap! They *were* going to try to run me down.

Somewhere in the distance, I heard my mother scream my name.

The car veered to the left, anticipating that I would turn back and run as that side was closer, but I sprinted to the right. Ahead of me was the town park and a few parked cars. I would have to cross through the park and a street to get to LC. No biggie, if not for the people in the way.

"Get back," I screamed. "Move away from the road." I gestured with my hands as I ran toward LC and away from them, drawing the car and any possible gunfire away from the moms in the park with their littles.

People scattered in all different directions, adding chaos to the scene and more worry for me.

Tires squealed behind me, and I glanced over my shoulder. The car had come to a screeching stop and was now backing up toward me, its white reverse lights bright.

I ran across the tip of the park, in front of the mini amphitheater, the flagpole, and small ice cream station someone had set up.

"Move back," I screamed. "Run away." I didn't know where to tell them to go to be safe because I didn't have any idea what this driver would do next.

A loud crash had me look over my shoulder. The car had backed into the flagpole which was teetering from the impact.

The car's engine revved, its tires squealed again as the driver peeled out while pointing the car in my direction.

The giant vehicle lurched forward, cutting a hard right, and drove over the exact spot I'd just run.

I hit the street, scanning for people. More people were closer to town and the buildings. Less were toward the waterfront and LC. I laser-focused on my destination, my SUV. I swerved closer to the cars parked near me, and seconds later heard the car clip those, knowing then there was no obstacle for this driver. I couldn't run between the cars because that left me to go up or down the road. Up was the town and people, down was the waterfront and open space. Nothing for me to hide behind.

I clenched my teeth. If this person wanted to play bumper cars, well then, so be it. I ran between the cars to the sidewalk, putting a row of vehicles between us but kept running toward LC.

The driver gunned his car, and just as I was reaching LC, the Mercedes driver swerved hard to the right and collided with LC's back end, shoving him at least two feet onto the sidewalk and nearly hitting me.

"Sam!"

I turned to see Leo running toward me, gun drawn. DB, the police chief, was not far behind him, though DB was running toward the intersection.

The Mercedes backed up and rammed LC again, shoving him even farther onto the sidewalk.

Man, it pissed me off that this butthead was trashing my car. I loved LC.

I hood-slid across LC to the driver's side while the Mercedes was backed up again, preparing for another ramming. I fumbled to get the key in the ignition, getting it on the second try and fired up LC. I threw the gear shifter in reverse and floored it. Looking over my shoulder to the Mercedes, I turned the steering wheel and aimed for the vehicle's front end. I braced myself for impact.

We collided. Hard. I pitched forward, hitting my head on the steering wheel, but managed to stay alert. Blood trickled down toward my eye. I threw the gear shifter into drive, moved forward a few feet, then put the car in reverse again. This time, I took a second to strap on my seat belt.

The Mercedes engine revved, and with my foot on the brake I did the same. Man, car makers knew what they were doing all those years ago when they made these vehicles like tanks.

I shot backward, but before hitting the Mercedes, I jerked the wheel and slammed the car into drive, wanting to draw him away from town. LC's engine whined, and he made a weird scraping sound as I lurched forward and drove down the road to the waterfront. The Mercedes, its front end hanging slightly askew, followed. I went about ten yards, the Mercedes gaining speed as it moved to catch me.

My cell phone chimed with a text, but I ignored it. Instead, I slammed on my brakes.

The impact of the collision broke out the back glass from LC's cargo door.

In my rearview mirror, I saw DB take a knee in the middle of the street and aim his gun at the Mercedes. Two shots later, and the driver's back tire popped.

The Mercedes gunned its engine, and the force of it started pushing me down the steep road.

DB took another shot and blew out the passenger back tire. This did nothing to dissuade the driver. But I noted that he wasn't firing back. Leo was running up to the Mercedes, and there was no return fire.

LC began to slide down the road slowly, his engine grinding as I pressed hard on the brake. Then it dawned on me to let go, I jammed the gear shift into neutral. I would hit the flat part of the road before the Mercedes and that gave me an advantage.

I let the Mercedes push LC with one hand on the gear shift as I waited for the road to level out. The second it did, I threw the car into drive and punched the gas. LC shot forward with a squeal of tires and smoke. I went just far enough to give me two-car lengths' distance before jerking the wheel and doing a one-eighty-degree spin. I faced the Mercedes, which was now just hitting the flat part of the road, and I floored it. Wincing as I drew in closer to the car. I knew he would floor his vehicle, too, and I planned for that move.

And I'd planned well.

I T-boned the Mercedes. Dead-on. The impact of which was going to leave some serious bruising across my body from the seatbelt and a bad case of whiplash. My shoulder screamed, and it felt like I'd pulled the stitches. But say what you want about old cars, the lack of airbags in this case had given me an advantage. Though I sure would have liked one for this last hit.

Steam erupted from both LC and the Mercedes. Leo was on the other car in seconds. Pulling open the passenger door and yanking someone out.

I leaned back in my seat and pressed a hand to my forehead.

DB was at my window. "You know this character?"

"No," I said. "Never seen him before."

"Well, I'm thinking he knows you, and he doesn't like you much."

"Something the two of you will have in common when you question him." DB and I went all the way back to elementary school. He'd been one of the kids to tease me when I struggled to read and then later cheated off me in chemistry.

I reached for my seat belt.

"Nope," DB said. "Stay still. Ambulance is on the way."

"I'm okay," I said.

"Yeah, I'm sure you are, but we're going to do this by the book. I don't need your dad writing me up in his paper about poor responses and care. I have an election coming up."

I groaned. "My dad. I bet he and my mom saw the whole thing."

So much for not stressing my dad out.

CHAPTER TWENTY-FIVE

I PRESSED THE ICE PACK TO MY FOREHEAD AND WINCED.

Tupi Whitehorse continued to shine the light in one eye and then the other.

"How much longer are you going to do that?" I asked.

He tucked the penlight away. "I was getting worried when you weren't complaining. And you swear you didn't lose consciousness?"

"I would shake my head, but movement hurts. No, there wasn't time."

He gently pressed his fingers around my neck, moving from muscle to muscle. "Hurt?"

"Aches more than hurts. You aren't going to make me go to the hospital, are you?"

"He should," Leo said, coming up to where I sat in the back of the ambulance.

"I really wish he would," my mom said, wringing her hands. Dad stood quietly to the side, hands in his pockets.

"Sorry about your salad," I said.

He gave a gallant shrug. "Once this is over, I'm getting a

burger. I think after watching that, I earned a burger." His tone dared my mother to say otherwise.

"How can you joke at a time like this, Russ. That man was trying to kill our daughter." Mom shifted her weight to her other foot and sighed.

"He wouldn't be the first," Dad said. He moved to Mom and placed a hand on her shoulder. "What you should be saying is look how adeptly she handled that guy, Elizabeth. I'm so proud of her. I wish she weren't in these situations, but when she is, she's a rock star."

I smiled. "Thanks, Dad." I turned to Leo. "What do we know about this guy?"

Leo crossed his arms and watched Tupi assess me. "Nothing yet. No ID. No registration on the car. Oliver took the perp back to the jail and is running prints."

Oliver Gee was one of the three patrol officers for Wind River. He had a kind heart, and a perseverance similar to a dog with a bone. If he was running down who the driver was, I felt confident he wouldn't rest until he had something.

DB ambled up to the ambulance. "Nice driving there, Sam. You could be a stock-car racer."

My mom groaned. "Don't give her any ideas, DB."

"Nice shooting, Dweebie," I said, using the childhood nickname we had for him. Nickname aside, I was very grateful for his shooting, and I made sure my tone reflected that.

His lips twitched with what might have been the hint of a grin. DB and I really didn't get along that well. He still harbored a grudge against me for proving my innocence when he'd arrested me last year for the murder of the local principal. He didn't like being bested. Which I'd done royally.

"You sure you don't know this joker?" He jerked his thumb in the direction of the car where the driver had been, though he'd long ago been hauled off to jail.

"No, and before you ask, I've never seen the car before either."

"Any recent suspicious activity, something that you might think is nothing, but now stands out?" DB asked.

Leo and my dad snorted.

DB put up a hand. "Never mind. I forgot who I was talking to. Listen, as soon as Tupi clears you, I want to see you at the station. We're not done here."

"Okay," I said. My phone vibrated and chimed in my bag. I pulled it out. On the screen were five missed calls. Four from Caleb, the latest from Toby. A series of text messages from Caleb read:

> **CALEB**
>
> Where are U?
>
> I'm getting really freaked out here. What if there are new bugs?
>
> Hello????????
>
> OMG, this was in my medicine cabinet.

Next was a picture of Nessa's prescription bottle for Warfarin. My blood went cold.

> I'm scared to be here. Scared to leave.

That was the last text from Caleb.

I texted Toby. It was high time for him so asking him to come get me was a long shot and probably not the best plan, but Leo was going to be tied up, and my parents weren't going to help with much, not after what they just witnessed.

> Can you come get me. Dad's newspaper. ASAP.

TOBY

> OMW

On my way.

Weird to get such an immediate response and action.

"Sam, did you hear me? Straight to the police station." DB's voice was hard and firm.

"Okay, but it might be a while. Tupi said he wanted me to go to the hospital, right Tupi?"

Tupi had been taking my pulse; he glanced up at me. His eyes narrowed slightly. "Yeah, I'd love it if you went. Just to rule out a concussion."

I smiled at DB. "As soon as I get cleared, I'll come right to you."

He watched me for a second and following a nod, strolled off.

My dad said, "Well, if you're going to get checked out, we should come with you."

Leo shook his head. "She's not going to the hospital, Russ. Something else is going on."

I explained about Caleb and how Toby was on the way.

"What about your concussion?" Mom asked.

Tupi said "I don't think she has one. But she's going to be pretty sore the next few days. She'll need to stay with someone or have someone stay with her just in case."

"I got her," Leo said. He met my gaze. "You go see what's

up with this Caleb kid, and then you come straight to the station. If I don't see you in a few hours, I'll put out an APB."

"Deal," I said with a smile. "Thanks for your help today."

He nodded, stepped up to me, and dropped a lingering kiss on my temple. "Sometimes it would be easier for me if you just ran to the police or hid in your house. But then again, I never really did like easy. You were pretty badass back there."

I squeezed his hand. "I'll keep you in the loop with any changes."

"Nope," he said with a chuckle. "No changes. Caleb, then station."

"Okay," I said. "Can you get the bobblehead out of LC. It's bugged. It needs to be somewhere where it can't eavesdrop."

Leo paused, watching my face a second, looking for who knows what.

"A bugged bobblehead?"

"Never a dull moment," I said

He nodded once, then went to LC to clean it out before heading to the station.

Tupi bandaged the cut over my eye where I'd slammed my head into the steering wheel. He held out two tablets.

"Typically, I don't do this. They would do this at the hospital, but you're gonna have a wicked headache. Take some meds now."

Toby's Prius pulled to the curb. He unfolded his lanky frame from the car.

"Jeez, what happened here?"

Tupi pointed to me. "You need to watch her. Any changes in speech, confusion, intense headache, you take her right away to the hospital. Do not pass go—"

"Do not collect two hundred dollars, yeah, yeah, I get it." He turned toward me. "You did all this?" He gestured to the carnage of damaged cars.

I nodded. "I had some help. Someone tried to run me down."

"And Sam said, no thanks, with her hammer." Tupi said.

Toby shook his head. "Your hammer looks like it might not make it." He pointed to LC where the tow truck guy was hooking him up to take him away. LC did look to be in bad shape.

"If they decide to come after you in my car, we're goners." Toby swallowed hard.

"We're only going down the street. We should be okay." I mentally crossed my fingers. What happened next was anyone's guess.

We were at Caleb's in minutes, and I slowly climbed the three flights up, my hips and chest aching from being tossed around in the car. I groaned, and Toby faced me.

"You okay?"

"A little sore, it's setting in."

"Want something to take your mind off it?"

"Sure," I said with a smile.

"Precious is off the grid."

I paused. "What? What do you mean 'off the grid.'"

He was two steps ahead, and he stopped. "I've been trying to call her. Her voice mail says that the offices are closed until further notice. I went to her website, and it says she's no longer taking clients at this time, and her contact page is gone."

I'd left my messenger bag in Toby's car but had tucked my phone in my back pocket. I whipped it out and dialed Precious.

After three rings it went to voice mail. "I don't like this."

"Should we go to her instead?"

I really wanted to. "Let's do this real quick and then go find her." I dug deep for the strength to stay the course and pushed back Toby as I took the stairs two at a time. At Caleb's door, I rapped hard twice but didn't wait for a response. He said he was scared. I rapped again and yelled his name. When he still didn't answer, I picked the lock and entered.

"Caleb, it's Sam," I called out to what my gut told me was an empty apartment. I walked through and pictured how it looked when I'd been there earlier.

His computer was in place. His closet door was ajar, and upon inspection, I saw a few empty hangers. Likely a coat missing.

In his bedroom, some drawers were askew, as if he'd packed in a hurry. On the counter in his bathroom were Nessa's meds. Using the sleeve of my shirt, I picked up the bottle. It had been filled with thirty pills one week ago. I opened the bottle, and there were only eight pills remaining. The bottle should have been full. I put the meds back on the counter and stepped back. I needed to compare this bottle with the one in Nessa's medicine cabinet to make sure they were one and the same. But if memory served, the bottle at Nessa's had been filled almost forty-five days ago.

Caleb's toothbrush and toothpaste were gone. As was his razor.

"He's bolted. We have to find out where. But first, Precious." I snapped some quick pictures with my phone, then headed to the front door. I didn't get past the kitchen before I blacked out.

CHAPTER TWENTY-SIX

I woke up on a couch in a place that looked vaguely familiar though I couldn't reason out how I got there.

The dark, masculine leather furniture. The woven and beaded throw pillows. A large eagle done in Native American art hung over the fireplace.

"Leo?" I pushed on the couch cushions trying to sit up. My body, especially my head, groaned in protest.

Leo and Tupi came into the living room, coffee mugs in their hands.

"How did I get here?" I asked Leo. Here being his house.

"You don't remember?" Tupi asked.

"I remember being in Toby's car and then Caleb's apartment and..." Flashes of memory came to me. "I think I passed out. I got dizzy all of a sudden." I pointed at Leo. "Then you were there, and we were getting into your car, and I don't remember coming here. I guess I have a concussion."

Tupi shrugged. "Or shock or both. You think you'd be used to trauma by now, but I guess your body is still figuring out how to respond. If you want to rule things out, you could go to the hospital for a scan."

I shook my head, though only slightly, as movement hurt. "What did you tell DB?"

"That you passed out and that it would be a while before you showed up."

I leaned back onto the couch. "Where's Toby? I need to find Precious and this kid Caleb. He's missing. He doesn't have a car, so I want to check Addie and all the private drivers in the area at the time."

Leo handed me his mug. "Drink up. Toby is already working on Caleb's ride. Your dad has been dispatched to Precious."

I stiffened and pushed against the couch to sit back up. "My dad? What does he know—"

"Nothing. He thinks you're working with Toby on this Caleb case. We mentioned a little of what Precious was going through, and your dad, having been sued by the professional football organization for his exposé about drugging, all those years ago, figured he had some real-world experience that might come in handy for Precious right now."

I eased back again and closed my eyes. The mug soothingly warm in my hand. "Yeah, that's a good move."

"For now, all you have to do is put the bat signal out so we can find Carson. I have some stuff to share with him." Leo sat on the couch next to me.

"Well, this is where my expertise is no longer needed," Tupi said. "Leo, I'll see you at the tribal meeting. Sam, I'll see you ... well, I hope I don't see you in my rig soon. Just see you out casually like at the store or something."

I opened my eyes and smiled at him. "That sounds like a solid plan." To Leo, I said, "I have no idea how to reach

Carson. He just shows up when I really don't want him to. So the fact that we want him... Wait, did you try Toby?"

"Yes. He's got nothing."

My phone rang. It was my dad.

"Hey," I said.

"Precious isn't at her house or her office, and I called her dad. He hasn't seen her today. Any ideas?" He sounded worried.

"Did everything look okay at her house?"

"Do you mean did her house looked tossed? No. More like she was out of town or something."

"I don't know where she could be. I mean, if she was in trouble or something, I'd hope she'd come to me." If she couldn't come to me, then where would she go? "Try AJ. I can send you his info. Or I can call him."

"No. Don't tip her off. If she's having a moment and trying to avoid people, that will include me. Besides, I have AJ's info. You gave it to me when you were working his case."

I pressed two fingers to my throbbing temple. "Okay, let me know what you find."

We disconnected, and I worked on steadying my breath, hoping it would ease the pain in my head.

"After Nessa died, I looked through her house for her pill bottle. It was in her medicine cabinet. Then today it popped up at Caleb's. And now he's missing. A man tries to run me down, and Precious is missing. Why aren't the dots connecting?" I rolled my head to the side to look at him, bringing the coffee to my mouth. The hot liquid was very soothing. "Can you bring me my phone? I need to see if the pill bottles match."

He went for my purse. "Lora said their first PI thought

Caleb was their stalker. You don't think so. But could you be wrong? I ask myself this question all the time when I'm investigating a crime and have my assumptions or beliefs."

I sipped more coffee before I answered. "Sure, I could be wrong, but he doesn't make sense. Someone sent Lora and Caleb spyware. Would he do that to throw me off? Sure. But I don't think so. Someone, maybe the same person, but I don't think so, bugged Lora's office, I suppose Caleb could have ridden his bike over there and done it. Again, could be that he's an excellent liar. And he bugged his own house for show. And now his text about finding Nessa's meds. Yeah, it could be one really good con. But what about the Shadow Man? What about Caleb not using the same VPN the stalker used. How does he get poison in the mochi? He has opportunity to get it in the boba tea, but not the mochi."

"What did the PI say when you told him today?"

I adjusted and winced as my body ached with the movement. "That's the thing. He didn't believe me. At first, I thought maybe he was ticked that I'd done something he'd been hired to do. I turned over my info on Winnie Dunlap." My eyes went wide. "Winnie Dunlap. We need to get someone to her. I believe she was stalking Lora, stealing keystrokes. Maybe she knows something more."

Leo sat up. "Winnie Dunlap?"

I nodded. I didn't like the look on his face; it screamed trouble.

"Winnie Dunlap was in a car accident about an hour before your attempted hit and run. She's in critical condition at the hospital."

I jerked upright. "What happened?"

"She ran off the road and clipped a pole, flipping a few times."

"Was she alone?"

Leo nodded and took my mug from my hands. "I'm guessing you want your hospital visit now?"

I nodded and stood. "Get someone to Addie's house. She planted the spyware. She might have even delivered the bug. And she knows Winnie. Said she was applying to work for her now that Nessa was dead."

Leo picked up his phone, then handed me my messenger bag and shoes. We were in his truck in under five minutes. Oliver Gee was dispatched to Addie's apartment.

I found the initial picture of Nessa's meds and compared it to the picture taken at Caleb's. They were not the same. One had been filled three weeks before the other and at a different pharmacy.

CHAPTER TWENTY-SEVEN

AT THE HOSPITAL, LEO FLASHED HIS BADGE, WHICH
made everything a hundred times easier. We were given
Winnie's room number. She was in the intensive care unit.
When we reached the barrier that separated the rest of the
hospital from the ICU, Leo held his badge up to the window,
and the nurse buzzed him in. But before that she held up one
finger, indicating only one of us could enter.

With one hand on the door, he said, "Trust me, I'll ask all
the questions you would want me to ask."

I nodded, frustrated that I would always have to find
other creative paths to get the answers Leo was going to get
in five minutes.

I paced the hallway, waiting for him to exit, checking my
phone. The elevator chimed, and I glanced up, more due to
reflex than actual curiosity.

Addie stepped out. Her head hung low, she wore a ball
cap, and she fidgeted with a hospital visitor pass.

She walked to the ICU door and paused, digging in her
purse.

From behind her I said, "Addie?"

She jumped, squealed, and spun to face me. Eyes wide with panic, and frozen in place, she looked like a deer in the headlights.

"You okay?" I asked. I kept my voice low and soft and lifted a hand, palm up, to encourage her to stay.

"Where did you come from?"

"I was standing back there. Waiting for my boyfriend to come out of the ICU. He's the cop talking to the desk nurse."

She glanced over her shoulder, nodded, then faced me again.

"Do you know what happened?" I asked.

She shook her head. "Not really." A lone tear rolled down her face.

I gestured to the bench that sat midway down the hallway. "Want to wait with me? When Leo comes out, he can tell you what he knows."

Addie didn't move. Her breathing was shallow, her face pale. Something more was happening here. I surveyed her body; she didn't look hurt. I studied her face; her pupils were dilated. She might be in shock. I took a step toward her. She flinched.

"Addie," I said. "You seem scared. But I'm here. I'll protect you."

"Like you protected Caleb?" Her voice was but a whisper.

And the next piece of the puzzle clicked in place for me. Caleb had fled ... to Addie. He didn't have a car, and he was smart enough not to use a private hire car when he knew he was being watched.

"Is Caleb okay?"

"What do you care? He asked for your help, and you never showed up."

I pointed to the bandage on my head. "I was in a car accident trying to get to Caleb." I lifted my shirt slightly to show the already ugly bruising I'd gotten from the seatbelt.

Addie gasped, and a flood of tears were unleashed. "Who is doing this to us?"

I gestured for her to come to the bench. I eased down, not bothering to hide my wincing. "I don't know, but the guy who did this to me is in custody, and when I find out who he works for, there will be hell to pay."

Addie watched me, then after a few beats, she came to the bench and slowly sat. "I was supposed to be with Winnie."

I rolled her words around for a second. "You mean when she was in her accident you were supposed to be with her in the car?"

Addie nodded. "But Caleb had come running over to my apartment. He was really scared. He asked me to take him somewhere, to hide him."

Her breathing was still ragged and choppy. It was clear that retelling this story was painful. I paused to let her gather her wits before continuing.

"Poor Caleb. He's just as much a victim as Nessa. I tried to protect him, but I failed him too."

"Tried to protect him by putting spyware on his computer?" I made sure to keep accusation out of my voice.

She shook her head. "That was Winnie. She was so jealous of Lora. She wanted to steal her gaming moves. It's my fault Caleb was sent the picture. I told Winnie how Lora and Nessa liked Caleb and trusted him, so she watched Caleb too."

She shook her head and wiped away tears with the heel of her hand. "It's crazy and doesn't make sense. If they trusted Caleb so much, why would they believe Walt?" She stared at me, her eyes large. "You know he said Caleb was their stalker. I heard him telling Lora and Nessa to file a restraining order. To build a case to put him in prison. Can you believe that? Caleb? Never. He's the sweetest, kindest guy I've ever met."

That's when I saw what Addie had been trying to hide. She had a crush on Caleb. "Is that why you helped Winnie put spyware on Caleb's computer? Because you thought he was being wrongly accused?"

"And I wanted to prove that Caleb wasn't the stalker. But he used a VPN, and the stalker did too. At least that's what Winnie said."

"Winnie was helping you try to find the stalker?"

She shook her head. "Winnie said she would try to help me. That's how she convinced me to put on the spyware, but Winnie really wanted to hack into Lora's game strategy. Winnie knew more about computers than I did, and I asked her to trace the emails. That's when she told me about the VPN. If I couldn't figure out who the stalker was, I thought maybe Lora and Nessa would get distracted by losing some games and not worry about Caleb. But they never lost."

"So if Winnie didn't keep up her end of the deal and try to find the stalker, why were you even talking to her about working for her?"

Addie used the hem of her shirt to wipe her tears. "I wasn't. I was trying to get her to keep looking. But she was mad because she wasn't getting the info from Lora's computer that she needed. She'd only had access to Lora's gaming computer for one game before Nessa died."

"You were the one who manually installed it. Why did you wait so long? Lora had opened the email with the picture a few weeks earlier."

"I never had a chance. Lora never left that gaming computer logged in. But she did a few weeks ago when she heard Walt and Nessa going at it." Addie closed her eyes and gave into her tears.

I let her release all the feelings before asking the next question. "And you and Winnie were supposed to meet today?"

Another nod. "She got a call from one of the potential sponsors about a meet and greet. They asked her to come. She thought they might be rekindling their interest in her, now that... you know... Nessa is gone, and Lora..."

"And you were going with her?"

"They told her it was okay to bring her assistant, so she asked me to come. She said maybe that lie we told you about me working for her wasn't such a bad idea. That we could talk about it on the ride. But then Caleb showed up, and I told her I'd meet her there. Next thing I know, I'm sitting in traffic, trying to get to the venue. When I got to the scene of the accident, I saw Winnie's car. How many other hot pink MINI Coopers are there in the county? None."

"Where's Caleb?"

"At my parents'. They're out of town for the week at a home improvement show. My dad does bathroom remodels."

The door to the ICU opened, and Leo stepped out. There was a haggard look on his face. I stood. Addie choked back a sob.

"It's bad, isn't it?" she cried.

"Hey, this is Addie. She was meeting Winnie when she

saw the accident. She was supposed to be in the car but wasn't able to meet up because she was helping Caleb hide."

Leo nodded once, then sighed heavily, then squatted before Addie. "Listen, Addie. Your friend sustained some very serious injuries. She's on life support, her brain activity isn't there. The nurse said she's alive because of the machines. Winnie's parents have decided to take her off life support, but because Winnie wanted to be an organ donor ,they are going through that process to find the appropriate candidates. I'm sorry."

Addie buried her head in her hands and sobbed.

From his back pocket, Leo took out his cell phone and showed me a text.

OLIVER GEE

No ID yet on Sam's attacker. But talked to Clark County sheriff, and video footage shows the MINI Cooper being sideswiped and run off the road. They're calling it a hit and run and have a BOLO for the car.

He gestured for me to scroll down. After the message there was a screenshot of the police report of Winnie's accident. I scanned the details.

I returned his phone and pressed a hand to my aching temple. For someone to sideswipe Winnie at just the right spot, so she hit an embankment, flipped, and went over a railing, into a ravine— this person knew what they were doing. This was deliberate.

I put an arm around Addie. "Hey, I'm sorry," I said.

"You're going to think I'm a terrible person. I'm sad about Winnie but relieved that I wasn't in the car." Her expression reflected her pain and confusion.

"I'm glad you weren't there too. And I'm glad that you

helped Caleb. Now let me help you. We need to keep you both safe."

Addie was a smart girl. Something in my words tipped her off. "Are you saying what happened to Winnie wasn't an accident?"

"I don't know for sure, but I don't like it. I'm going to get to the bottom of this."

Leo touched her knee to draw her attention. "I'm going to take you into protective custody. You and Caleb. Are you okay with that?"

Addie paled. "Yes."

Leo turned toward me. "What's the plan?"

"I'm going to have Toby come get me. You take her, and get Caleb. I'm going to chase down a few leads she gave me."

"Me?" Addie said and pointed to herself.

"What company called you, and where was the venue?"

Addie pulled her phone out and showed me a screenshot from Winnie.

"Can you airdrop that to me?"

She did.

"Once I've run this down, I'll come to the station."

Leo stood and wrapped his arms around me. "Please, watch your back."

"I will," I said against his neck and breathed him in.

We slowly pulled apart, knowing this is when things had the opportunity to go sideways and who knew what could happen.

I texted Toby and asked him to pick me up.

Addie stood and told Leo she was ready to go.

"Wait, one quick question," I asked. "If you had spyware on the computers, why did Winnie bug the bobbleheads?

The spyware let you listen in and see in through the computers."

Addie looked confused. "I don't know what you mean about bugging the bobbleheads. Those were from Walt, or, well... more like Catherine. She thought they were cute."

CHAPTER TWENTY-EIGHT

WHILE STANDING OUTSIDE THE HOSPITAL WAITING FOR Toby, I checked my phone. No messages from either Dad or Precious.

Agitated at finding none, I struggled to not let my imagination run away with me, though it was hard when everyday life showed me how awful people could be to each other.

I pondered what Addie had said about the bobbleheads being from Catherine. Obviously, that didn't mean she stuck the bug in each one of them. Anyone could have broken in and placed the bugs in the funky toy. Where I was hung up was the bobbleheads going missing. If a person breaks in to plant a bug, why break back in to take the bug? Why take the items the bugs were hidden in? And here's the other thing, Lora's bobblehead was gone, but not Caleb's. Whoever planted the bug was still wanting info from Caleb.

Toby pulled up and made a quick rocking stop. When I opened the door, he blurted out, "Hurry, get in. Your mom is headed this way."

I slid into the car, ignoring the aches and pains that

screamed each time I moved. "Why is Mom here? Is my dad okay? Precious?"

"Haven't heard anything yet. She's here getting your dad some more meds. The pharmacy in town was out." He didn't wait for my door to close fully before peeling out. "Well, that's what your dad told her. He said she needed a task while he was out looking for Precious, or she would just sit at home and worry about you and him."

I felt bad about running from my mom, but if she saw me here, she'd just get more worried, considering the last she heard I was okay and didn't need to come to the hospital.

I slunk low in the seat until we were out of the hospital lot and headed toward the interstate. That's when a piece of the puzzle clicked into place.

"Wait. How is it my mom is able to get Dad some more meds when he just had the prescription filled, and why is she allowed to pick them up?"

"All she has to do is show proof, like your dad's driver's license and a note from him or something to get them. And he had his doctor call in a second prescription, said he lost the others." Toby was clutching the steering wheel, his eyes darting between the road ahead and the road behind.

"Are you worried we're being followed?"

"I'm worried about everything. That Caleb kid missing, you passing out, the bumper car derby event earlier—"

"The Caleb kid is found. Leo is on his way to get him. Go back to the prescription. Let me ask you something. Because of HIPPAA, there is no way we can find out legally if Nessa had a second prescription filled, like my dad is doing. And we won't know who picked it up or anything, right?"

"You said legally, right? Because all that would require

would be a confession or a warrant. I can try to hack into the system, but I doubt we'll know who picked up the stuff unless we can narrow down a time and place, then we can watch the video if they still have store footage."

"But we don't have the time for that. Someone killed Winnie and was hoping to get Addie too. Someone planted Nessa's pills at Caleb's. Someone tried to kill me. What I don't know is if the attempt on me is connected to the others or part of the hit. But what I do know is that things are accelerating."

"Where do we start first?"

"Well, this is where I tell you that you don't have to come with me. That you can drop me off at a car rental place or something, and I'll get a car. You can do whatever I need from the safety of your home."

"Going home sounds very attractive; I'll admit it. I'm off my schedule, and I don't like being off my schedule. I need my high time. I need that time to reset, and because I haven't had it, I can't shake the feeling that everything is off. That something bad is going to happen."

I snorted. "I have that feeling even when things are going right."

"I'm not going to drop you off anywhere, even if I am tempted to give you the keys to my car and go hide. So where to?"

"Lora. Take me to Lora."

"I'm glad Lady M isn't with us. I'd hate for her to get hurt."

"No one is going to get hurt," I said with not a lot of confidence. Maybe I should say no more people are going to get hurt, but that was just wishful thinking.

I checked my phone again, looking for information from

anyone, only to find nothing. I worked with a team. I needed others to help me. As much as I'd fought that fact, there it was. I could pretend all I wanted that Toby just did computer stuff for me, but he did far more than that. Same with Leo and Precious. Yet, when I didn't know where Precious was, much less her state of mind, or how Leo was faring, I couldn't help but feel that my team wasn't together.

I chewed on my thumbnail and checked the little pocket I clipped into the inside of my pants waist. The little pocket that kept spare handcuff keys, a mini pocketknife, and an Apple Airtag so Leo could locate me if I went missing. Which *had* happened in the past, that's why I wore it.

"Sam," Toby said.

I jerked my head toward him, afraid of what I would find. Only there was nothing. Just Toby smiling at me.

"When this is all done, maybe you should have a high time. You're wound supertight. I can feel you vibrating from here. It's messing with my own energy, so knock it off. We've been here before, and we've always come out okay. We'll do it again this time too. We're together, and that's what counts."

"Precious," I said and looked out the window. My eyes a little moist from his words.

"She'll be okay. She always has been. This time is no different."

I nodded once. "I feel like it's been quiet too long. Like something might be wrong."

"Nah, this is just a big moment for her. This won't come between the two of you; you're too solid for that."

He was right. We were solid. Like Nessa and Lora had been. Which made me wonder if Toby felt like the odd man out sometimes, kinda like Addie had. That's when the solution popped into my head. I could now see the next steps of my plan.

"Do you have any paper?"

"In the front pocket of my computer bag. Why?"

"I have an idea. I need to write a script. There's spyware on Lora's phone, right?"

"Yeah."

"If we take her phone, then the person is spying on us, right?"

"Again, yeah."

I busily scratched out my script as Toby drove.

He pulled up to the curb outside Lora's house and turned the car off. "You ready?"

"Yeah," I showed him the script.

He smiled in understanding. "Let's go. Let's end this."

"Grab your computer. We're gonna need it."

We exited the car and were on Lora's parents' porch when she opened the door.

"What's happened?" She looked between me and Toby.

"Is there someplace we can talk?" I nodded toward the news van that was also parked along the curb. The reporter was jogging toward us.

Lora gestured for us to hurry into the house and closed the door in the reporter's face.

"I'd say we go outside, but I wouldn't put it past them to eavesdrop. Have a seat." She showed us to the living room.

I stood but waited for Lora and Toby to sit. I was too high-strung to sit. Yeah, Toby was right, my vibe was tightly wound.

Toby opened his computer and waited.

"Let me see your phone," I said to Lora.

She pulled it from her hip pocket and handed it to me. I

took it into the guest bathroom, wrapped it in a towel and put it in the cabinet. Because I was extra paranoid.

"What's that about?"

"I'll explain in a bit, but first, Winnie Dunlap was contacted by a person named Verna Willen from that kids' streaming service. They asked her to join them at a venue in Vancouver."

Lora's brow furrowed. "Here? In town? That's odd. What do they have going on in town?"

I shrugged and gestured for Toby to find the answer to that question. I showed him the screenshot I got from Addie.

I turned back to Lora and took a seat next to her on the couch. "On the way to this venue, Winnie was in an accident. She did not survive." I explained how Winnie's parents were fulfilling her wish to be an organ donor.

Lora clapped a hand over her mouth, and tears streamed down her face.

"Addie was supposed to be with her."

Lora paled, still unable to speak.

"Yes, I think Winnie was killed. Winnie had keylogging spyware put on your laptop. She wanted to know your gaming strategy. She used Addie to help her."

"But Addie? We've been friends forever. Why would she do something like that?"

"Caleb. She has a crush on him, and she knew that Walt was accusing him of being your stalker. She thought Winnie could help her figure out who the real stalker was. Winnie thought she could figure out your strategy through keystrokes. Winnie really wanted what you and Nessa were putting together."

"Was Winnie the one who hurt Nessa?"

"I don't think so. She used Addie to get to you. She didn't

break into your house, but I can't say that for sure because of how you used the codes. Plus, Winnie is dead. Someone wanted her out of the picture. I don't know why yet. But I have a sneaking suspicion that if we were to go to her place, we could find evidence that she is responsible for the spyware and the stalking."

Lora shook her head. "I don't understand."

"I can't explain it because I don't have all the pieces yet to put together. I need your help to do that."

"Sure, anything."

"Tell me about Catherine."

Lora's expression showed her confusion. "Catherine? What do you want to know?"

"Did she ever pick up Nessa's meds? Go to her appointments with her?"

"She used to. But Nessa was really trying to cut the apron strings. Her mom was always pushing Nessa to do more, get more—more, more, more."

"More what?"

"More fame, I guess. She never said it outright, but it was pretty clear she didn't like that I was the face of the company and the sponsorship. She thought Nessa should at least be part of it all."

"But she was, right?"

Lora nodded. "Yeah. Nessa didn't want to be in front of the camera. Probably because her mom was such a camera hog. You know, she used to put Nessa in pageants and signed her up for all this child-acting stuff. Nessa hated it. She used to say she probably would be in front of the camera more if her mom pushed less. Catherine believed she never had the fame she deserved. I guess that's what drove her to push Nessa to it. It's really kinda sad."

"And Catherine knew where Nessa got her prescription filled and how much she took?"

"Yeah, of course. She was just as fanatical about the meds as she was about the recognition."

"Do you know if she ever had a prescription filled for Nessa?"

"You mean pick up one? Probably."

"How about recently?"

Lora shook her head. "Not that I know of. Though it's not hard. All she had to do was call Nessa's doctor and tell him she needed a refill."

"But if she just filled a prescription, how could they fill another one? Insurance only allows so much to be dispensed."

"We are mostly self-paid because we're self-employed. We don't have a great prescription plan. But one time Nessa lost a bottle of pills, maybe left them at a hotel while we were traveling. We never found them. Catherine called the doc and got a refill that day."

"How long ago was this?"

"I need my phone or laptop to access my calendar."

"I have it here," Toby said.

Lora scrolled through her calendar. "About a year ago. It was the trip to Boston. That's the first time we were approached by the streaming service."

"Was Catherine on that trip?"

Lora shook her head.

Highly unlikely Catherine took those meds back then. But maybe she knew from that incident how to get her hands on more medicine. Besides, the dates on the bottles were only three weeks apart.

Toby cleared his throat. "So, there is no venue, and this

email from Verna Willen, it's a spoof. The name on the email is Venna Willen, and because the font is small, the N and R blend, and it's hard to make out. The whole thing was a ruse."

"To draw Winnie and Addie out, to kill them," I said.

Lora put her hand on my arm. "And you think Catherine would want to kill them? That doesn't make sense. Why would Catherine want to kill Winnie or Addie or Nessa. Nessa was her only child. She would never hurt her."

"I don't think she wanted to kill Nessa. Nessa's death was an accident. An outcome Catherine never anticipated. And she's been trying to right that wrong ever since, only things keep getting worse. I think Catherine was trying to kill you."

CHAPTER TWENTY-NINE

I EXPECTED TEARS. HYSTERIA. LORA HAD BEEN through so much, and I'd hinted as much about how I believed she was the original target. But to learn the person targeting you was the mom of your best friend ... well.

That was a lot for anyone to take in.

"Tell me about Walt." Let's be honest. If Catherine really did this, she didn't do it alone. And Walt was the perfect person to spearhead this.

"Toby, pull up Walt's site again." I wanted to bang my head against the wall. Yeah, I was bothered by Winnie's accident, but not for all the reasons a regular person would be bothered. I knew my suspicious nature could skew my perception, but when I saw that Winnie had been run off the road and the car hadn't stayed at the scene, something hadn't felt right. Now I knew why.

I had all the pieces to the puzzle, and they were now starting to come together to make the perimeter.

"It's up," Toby said.

"Remember Paulie said Walt taught him defensive

driving? Does his site list defensive driving, and if so, who teaches it?"

Toby clicked around, then spun the computer so Lora and I could see the screen. "Walt teaches it. Says he has over thirty years of experience and even worked as a Hollywood stunt driver."

"That's how he met Catherine. They were on the set together. Nessa said that her mom always teased Walt about how he got into the PI business. It was because she hired him to catch Nessa's dad's affair in pictures. She was angling for a large settlement."

"Did she get it?" Toby asked.

Lora nodded. "But she never got a decent acting job again. And it drove her nuts. Did you know that Nessa's dad made a movie the year after they divorced and cast another actress who looked remarkably like Catherine as the lead. It was a blockbuster hit."

I caught Toby's eye. "Any weird accidents ever happen to Nessa's dad?"

Toby's fingers flew over the keyboard.

Lora sat back against the couch and closed her eyes. "I can't believe this is something we are even thinking."

"Tell me more about Walt. You started getting the emails, and Catherine suggested you bring Walt in, right?"

"Yeah. He got intense real fast. Talked about putting in a security system. Scanned the computers, like you did. Was really critical about our schedule. It was all very stressful. Nessa and I started to fight a lot. Until he said Caleb was our stalker and started talking about restraining orders and getting evidence together to 'nail him to the wall.'" She did air quotes. "It was disgusting, and Nessa and I knew then, we had to do something. That's when we came to you."

Toby cleared his voice. "Max Feldman, Nessa's dad, filed a few police reports a few months after his divorce from Catherine. Vandalism. Burglary. But then he amped up security, and that was that."

"How about the leading actress?"

Toby smiled. "I knew you were going to ask about her. She was in a serious car accident, a hit and run. She survived but had a spinal cord injury and never walked again. I pulled up the police report. It reads a lot like how you told me Winnie's accident went down. No one was ever apprehended."

To Lora I asked, "Are Walt and Catherine romantically involved?"

She shrugged. "They've never advertised that. But Nessa thought they were. Like friends with benefits or something. All I know is that they have a long history together."

My phone chimed with an incoming text.

DAD

Hey, Precious and I are at the paper. We hear you upstairs. Come down and join us. We have a surprise.

I showed the phone to Toby, who raised a brow. "Who's in your house?"

"That's what I'd like to know."

I texted Dad to say I'd be down as soon as I could, I didn't want him to come upstairs because I wasn't responding or because he knew that noise wasn't me. Then I texted the info to Leo.

I returned my attention to Lora. "I think this is all going to unravel soon, hopefully today. I can't shake the feeling that things are about to explode. Someone planted evidence on Caleb, tried to take me out, and killed Winnie. That would be a lot in a week ... but we're talking less than twenty-four hours. Don't go anywhere. Don't get online. You are ultimately the target. I am a barrier right now for you."

"So if something happens to you then..." Her eyes got wet with unshed tears.

"Yeah, then you're next. Don't let anyone in. Tell your parents everything." I handed her Leo's card. "This is the name of the detective that knows everything about me and your case. Call him if you need to." I flipped the card over and showed her the writing on the back. "This is the name of my lawyer. Tyson Lockett. If you want extra security, which I advise, then call him when I leave. Tell him who you are. He's expecting your call. He can hook you up with a private firm to provide security."

"You think I should do that?"

"I do. I think Nessa accidentally dying has probably further fed into Catherine's delusions about you holding back her daughter. If she blamed you before, she certainly blames you now. And I think she's very unpredictable. As is Walt."

"I just call this guy?"

"Yes, he's very trustworthy. I've put my life in his hands more than once."

She nodded, and a tear slipped down her face. "What a mess. Just a terrible—"

"Tragedy," I finished for her, then wrapped her in a hug. "I'm sorry. You did nothing wrong, but both you and Nessa have paid for someone else's jealousy and greed."

"Nessa paid the most."

"We'll get justice for her."

She hugged me back, sobbing against my shoulder. Just

as much as I was desperate to leave and get on with what was waiting for me at home, I knew Lora needed this. And I did too.

She pulled away and dried her eyes with her sleeve. "I guess I'll go fill my parents in and then call your friend."

"One more thing. This is going to be the hardest. I need to take your cell phone with me. You can use this." I handed her a burner phone Toby had. "Before we leave, Addie is going to call."

I showed Lora the script I'd written out and texted to Leo with instructions. "She's going to apologize. You just tell her that you aren't ready to talk to her right now. That you're headed to the police station and then your house to pick up a few things. Tell her you need time to process everything. As soon as you hang up, I'll take your phone, and we'll leave. Toby is then going to post online posing as you. Your phone has the spyware, which is why I removed it from this room and why we need to take it. I want whoever is tracking you to follow your phone. Keep your laptop shut. When this is all over, I'll return your cell phone."

"Clean of spyware, of course," Toby added. "Just stay offline altogether. I'm going to pretend to be you for a while."

"I can use the burner phone to call this guy?" She pointed to the card. "And how do I get in touch with you?"

"Yep, use that phone. You won't need to call me if you call Lockett. His men will let me know if I'm needed."

"Got it." She nodded. "Good luck."

I squeezed her hand. "Thanks." I nodded, and Toby began the first step in our plan. If I was right about Catherine and her bloodthirst for Lora, I believed I could push a few buttons to escalate her further. Plus, Lockett had his security team on standby, ready to protect. I just needed her to okay the invasion of privacy. And to understand the need.

I texted Leo that we were ready. Then I retrieved Lora's phone.

Moments later, Addie called.

I had hoped she wouldn't sound like she was reading from a paper, and she didn't, she was too broken up to sound anything other than sincere and scared.

Lora did great as well. We could only hope the call did the trick.

I gave Lora a reassuring smile as I took her phone, and we headed outside.

Once we were by Toby's car, he handed me his keys. "Be gentle."

I rolled my eyes. "I'm not planning on going off road or anything. "

"No, but it's not about what you plan, it's about what others have planned for you. And them wanting to do it to you when you're in my car."

"If we see anything suspicious you can shoot at them from your side of the car. That should help things." I opened the driver's side door and eased my aching body behind the wheel.

Toby got in next to me and opened his laptop. "Yeah, so that doesn't make me feel any better." He stroked his chest twice before realizing Lady M wasn't there.

Before we could pull away from the curb, a large dark SUV came to a screeching halt next to us, blocking me in.

Oh, no," Toby said. "That was quick."

The passenger door window rolled down, and Carson's face came into view. He was stretched across from the driver's side. "Come on, get in," he said.

I'd sprung him from the hospital yesterday, and he'd disappeared into the wind.

"Yeah! Carson, you're the man," Toby said and pumped his fist.

"You're just thankful we won't be in your car, aren't you?"

"More than words can express."

We switched from Toby's car to the SUV.

"How did you know?" I asked Carson as I climbed in the front passenger seat.

"Lockett and Leo. I talked to both and put some pieces together. If you're gonna pretend to be Lora moving around town, do it from behind a layer of tint that's hard to see through. Make them uncertain."

"Well. I would do it from LC, but that's not an option."

"Yeah, we're still trying to run that guy's identity down."

"You think he was part of the contract hit?"

Carson nodded as he checked the rearview mirror, then pulled into the street.

I turned around to Toby and gestured to the laptop. "Do your magic."

Because Toby had cloned Lora's laptop, he was able to now get in and pretend to be her. His first stop, a gaming chat room. He found the thread on Nessa and stoked the fires, posing as Lora and posting about how much *she* missed her best friend. About how so much had happened in the last week that *her* head was spinning.

Then Toby lowered the boom. Still posing as Lora he posted how her private investigator just came for a visit and told her about Winnie. How Winnie had tried to steal her keystrokes and begrudged her the potential sponsorship. But none of that mattered because Winnie had died today in a terrible car crash. Then Toby, still posing as Lora, planted the seed of a possible conspiracy.

When he was done, he sighed and sat back in the seat, watching the screen. "Okay. It's out there. I made sure to tag Walt and Catherine in case they have alerts set up." A second later his computer chimed.

"Aaannnnd, we're being tracked. They are now watching our moves."

"My dad says someone's in my apartment."

"Yeah, I got there a few minutes after they left. I was with Leo when your text came through. Your place has been tossed. The notes you had on the wall are gone. Your drawers emptied. I don't know if they found what they were looking for."

I remember how I'd shoved the photos of Lora's house under my couch. "Had the couch been moved or out of place?"

Carson shook his head.

Wow, pure dumb luck that they didn't look there, if the pictures were what they wanted. The bobblehead was at the police station. I couldn't imagine they were looking for anything else.

Carson drove us to the police station. Leo came out after I texted him and leaned in the window of the passenger door. He chin-nodded to Carson.

"We have a tail," Carson said. "Make sure to stay out of the sideview mirror, Sam, so they won't be tipped off."

"We're killing time," I told Leo. "That should give the person enough time to plant a trap at Lora's. Tell Addie she did great."

"Lora called Lockett," Leo said. "He said the security is in place. Caleb gave us permission to search his house. We have a team there now. Not only did they find Nessa's meds but also a series of emails from Winnie to Caleb conspiring to harm Lora."

"And the time stamps?" I didn't believe for a second they were real.

"All sent the same day, today. Someone did the basic altering of the emails. At first glance, they look like they were sent over a one-year period. But we had a tech guy go with us through the search, and he found the actual time stamp in no time."

"Trackable?"

He shook his head. "Used a VPN. We're going to get a warrant."

I smiled.

The keypad app on Lora's phone sent a notification. Someone had entered her home.

"Game on," Toby said.

I handed both Toby and Leo an earpiece. "This is where you get out, Toby. We can't have you in the car when we go in. You'll be a sitting duck."

"And what's it called when instead of being a sitting duck you run right toward the hunter like you're doing, Sam?"

"Payday," Carson said with a grin.

I met Leo's gaze and tried to hide my apprehension.

"I'll be five minutes behind you. Once your tail moves on, I'll follow. Be careful," Leo said. "And good luck."

CHAPTER THIRTY

We had to get to Lora's with enough time for the tail to not see Carson or me. The tail had to believe both Lora and I were in the car. While Carson drove, I strapped on a body-armor vest and zipped my hoodie up over it. I tucked a stun gun in my pocket and hid a small gun on my leg using an ankle holster. With Leo's help I was getting more proficient with firearms. I just didn't like to use them. Every time I pulled a trigger, I felt the seriousness of what that speeding bullet could do, the harm it could inflict.

We stopped and idled one street away from Lora's. Carson gave quick, short instructions and then was out the door and disappearing between the houses before I could get my seatbelt off.

My fingers fumbled with my messenger bag and Lora's phone as I rushed to get into the driver's seat. I drove the short distance to Lora's house and used her app to open her garage door. Then I eased the SUV partially in. I didn't want to get trapped. I was nervous about another car blocking me from behind as it was.

I got out, slammed the driver's door and for good measure, opened and closed the back passenger door as well. As if to imply two people were getting out of the car.

I paused at the door to the house, knowing this could be the trickiest part. I would be walking in blind. If someone were there ready to pick me and Lora off, I could only hope they'd aim for the chest and not the head.

I steeled my nerves, and thought that if my dad knew what I was doing, he'd surely have a heart attack—then opened the door.

I stood to the side and listened, though not for long because I worried about the tail we'd had. If he worked for me, I'd wait for him to drive by and verify. I didn't want their tail to tip our hand.

I stepped into the butler's pantry and strained to feel where a person might be. The comms were quiet. For a moment, I wondered if they could hear my heavy breathing.

"Leo's ETA is three minutes," Toby said quietly.

Yeah, I figured maybe they could. I pulled in a deep breath and tried to steady my nerves. I squared my shoulders, cleared my throat, and jumped right in.

To no one I said in a moderately normal voice, "Hurry and grab your things. I don't want to be here long." I stepped through the door from the butler's pantry into the kitchen.

A flash of steel to my right caught the sun and glistened, the cocking of a gun followed immediately, and I knew what was coming.

I had a decent idea of the direction and dove to my left just as the boom of the gun filled the kitchen, the burnt gunpowder assaulting my nostrils. A second later, I felt a slight punch to my lower back and knew the bullet had hit the vest. And it hurt.

Like *hurt* hurt. "Oh my God, that hurts," I said.

"Did it hit your vest?" Leo asked in a rush of words through the earpiece.

"Yeah, and it hurts."

"Real thing would have hurt worse," Carson said without sympathy.

What had I ever seen in him?

I flipped over on my back and tried to breathe through the pain. I put my hand on my back to feel for blood just in case I was wrong, but I came up empty.

Catherine ran toward me, stepped over me, her toe clipping my shoulder as she rushed to get to the pantry.

"Where is she?" Catherine screamed. "Where is that bitch?"

I eased up into a sitting position, my hands resting near my ankle. "You're looking at her."

"Heads-up." Carson said. "He's coming down the stairs toward you, Sam."

I glanced toward the stairs, not seeing Walt yet. I scooted across the floor on my butt to sit against the island, using it as a shield and removing myself from his direct line of site.

"What are you talking about?" Catherine waved the gun at me. Her hair was tangled and pulled into a haphazard ponytail. She wore no makeup, her eyes red and scanning the area wildly. "I want Lora! It's her fault my Nessa is dead."

"It's your fault," I said. "Yours and Walt's. Lora didn't put that poison in her drink or food. You did, or was it Walt?"

"Walt, but it was my idea." She smiled smugly.

"It was a bad one. It cost you everything." I knew better than to try and reason with a person who was so far removed from reality that they saw murder as a logical option. But I couldn't help but point out the obvious.

Catherine's smile fell. "Nessa didn't like mochi. Lora made her eat it."

"Lora was at the hospital. And Nessa did like mochi, that's why she ate it. I'm sorry Catherine. I'm sorry for your loss. But you did this, and you're still driven to do more harm, to kill Lora."

"She was holding back my girl. Nessa deserved the spotlight, and Lora was stealing it all."

"Did you ever ask Nessa what she wanted?" I continued to rub my back where it ached.

"I didn't have to. I know my child. I know what she wanted."

"You didn't even know she liked mochi. How much did you really know?" I hated twisting the knife, sorta. This woman's greed was the reason Nessa was dead.

"Shut up!" Catherine screamed. "Just shut up. I'm going to enjoy watching you bleed out."

"She's not going to bleed out," Walt said from behind me. "She's wearing a bulletproof vest. I told you not to use that gun, Catherine. But to let them come upstairs, and I would take care of them. We're lucky Sam here wasn't shot because how can we explain that to the cops? We have to make this look like an accident or a matter of choice. Not a homicide." He eased over to Catherine and took the gun gently from her.

"But what about Lora?" she whined.

"We'll get her, in due time."

I cleared my throat and sat still, not wanting to draw a negative reaction with any sudden movement. "Excuse me, but which one of you was the original stalker?" I looked between them both and settled on Catherine. "I think it was you. Am I right?"

She crossed her arms and looked away, but I knew I was right by the small smile that played on her lips.

To Walt, I said, "And you decided to frame Caleb, the odd hermit. I'll give you credit. He did make himself an easy target. But what I want to know is if you were the man waiting in the shadows, freaking him out most nights."

Walt tucked the gun, a small revolver, in an ankle holster, then reached behind me, grabbing me by the back of my shirt and vest.

"You ask a lot of questions. You think I don't know you're probably recording this or something? Rookie is what you are. Thinking I'd give you any type of confession." He jerked me up halfway and began to drag me across the floor toward the back door. "Well how about this for a confession? I'm going to get three million extra dollars just for drowning you in this pool out here."

I was facing the floor, sliding on my knees trying to get any type of purchase to right myself, my arms windmilling. But his words caught me cold.

Carson whistled in my ear. "Dirty rat," he said. "Sam, this guy runs two businesses, his PI firm and then this underground crime network, taking bribes for construction sites, credit card scams, chop shops, and gun for hire."

"Chop shops?" Leo said. "We found an association that your bumper-car driver is part of a chop shop in Washougal."

So today's car smashing was part of the hit, but for Walt, that was really two birds with one stone. How fortuitous for him that I had taken Lora's case. I went limp like a noodle, making it harder for Walt to move me. It worked. Walt staggered, caught off balance.

He dropped me as he went to catch himself.

I flipped over onto my back, and using the bottom corner of the island, I grabbed it and spun myself like a turtle, so my feet were close to him. I reared back like a braying donkey and kicked him square in the stomach. He doubled over.

"That's for being a dirtbag," I said.

I kicked him a second time in the man parts, using so much force I was pretty sure he was going to vomit on me from the pain.

Instead, his eyes went wide a second before his face went slack and he passed out, toppling over like a heavy tree.

"That's for taking the contract," I said while jumping to my feet.

"Ooh," Carson said. "I saw that kick. I can feel it from here."

"Did she kick him where I think she did?" Toby asked.

"Yeah, and he blacked out," Carson said.

Leo chuckled. "That's my girl."

"Put the knife down, Catherine," I said. Here I was again standing across the island from a person brandishing a knife at me. Only this time, I think things might not work out as well as they had with Caleb.

I touched the stun gun in my pocket. "Someone want to come get Walt while he's out?"

"I got him sighted," Carson said. "Deal with her, and I'll come in. She looks twitchy. I'm afraid if I come in, it'll spook her."

"We just apprehended the tail you guys had." Leo said. "I'm headed in through the garage, Sam."

"Catherine, put the knife down. So many people have already been hurt. Let's end this now. Tell me about Winnie."

"She was the perfect scapegoat, right? You know Walt didn't even know there was other spyware on Lora's devices until you pointed it out to him? How stupid can he be? He didn't even know Winnie existed really until you came along. So I guess you can thank yourself for drawing Walt's attention to her."

I would deal with that guilt later. "Why kill her? Why try to kill Addie?"

Catherine shrugged. "Too many loose ends, I guess. And if their deaths could cause Lora even more heartache, then wasn't that even better?"

Essentially, Catherine really was Lora's stalker. Only she didn't want to possess Lora like most stalkers wanted. She wanted to destroy her. She blamed Lora for everything she could, and that single-minded focus and obsession was very much stalker behavior. A stalker who escalated into a murderer.

Leo came up behind Catherine, quiet as a church mouse, and in a flash, he knocked the knife from her hand and had her arm twisted behind her so she couldn't move. All without drawing his gun.

"Catherine Siegel you are under arrest for the murder of Vanessa Taylor, Winnie Dunlap, and the attempted murder of Lora Darling and Addie Milner. I'm sure I'll find other charges to add to that."

Chief DB sauntered in and stopped at Walt's inert body. "Man's still out cold. We might need an ambulance here. At the very least an ice pack." He took a surveillance earpiece from his ear and placed it on the counter. "Nice job, Sam." He gave me a nod. "Now, you think you might want to come to the station so we can wrap this all up? I only asked for that hours ago."

"When did he get involved in this?" I looked to Leo for an answer.

"When you called about the script and we went to search Caleb's place. I didn't tell you because I knew you'd protest. The two of you are like oil and water." Leo cuffed Catherine. "Took a lot to convince him to let it play out the way it did. Both of you should be glad it ended like this."

"I'll need everyone to come to the station, now," DB said. He placed his hands on his hips. And in true DB fashion, he made his muscles pop up and down. And there was the DB I knew and expected. It didn't take long for him to always bring his focus back to himself. "And who was the other guy on the comms? He'll need to come in and give a statement, too."

"Uh," I said. "What other guy?" DB couldn't know Carson was alive. No one needed to know.

"You know the guy? The one who had sights on the PI here."

I shook my head. "I don't remember that."

I glanced at Leo. He ducked his head.

"Stillman?" DB asked Leo.

"You talking about Toby?"

"Why are you two gaslighting me?" DB asked. "I'm starting to get mad."

"Well, we can't have that. I hear steroid rage is not pretty," I deflected.

DB pointed a finger at me. "I don't take steroids. These are all natural muscles."

"Yep." I rolled my eyes.

The SUV in the garage roaring to life caught everyone's attention. Carson was making his getaway while the getting away was good.

DB pointed to the garage as he began walking in that direction. "Who is in the SUV?"

"Repo man?" I shrugged and skirted the island to cut him off. "Trust me, let this go."

He narrowed his eyes as he studied me.

"We got the bad guys. You're going to make national media because you caught the people who killed Nessa Taylor and uncovered a plot to kill a famous YouTube star. You should probably go by your house to change shirts, because you're going to be making lots of media statements."

This did the trick. DB returned his focus on himself. "Excellent point." He barked out a few commands and then exited the house to go home and find a shirt that flattered his eyes or something.

"Care to give a girl a ride to the station?" I asked Leo as I stepped up to him and dropped a quick kiss on his cheek, thanking him for letting Carson go. I needed Carson free and unexposed to help keep me alive.

"I'll even let you sit up front with me," he said with a wink.

"Gross," Catherine said.

CHAPTER THIRTY-ONE

We spent hours at the station giving our statements, repeating our statements, and then writing our statements. I was all statemented out and ready to go home. Lockett's security men had brought Lora down, and we filled her in on what had happened at her house. As expected, she broke down. She'd lost so much. Caleb and Addie surrounded her with love, as did her parents, and it seemed to help.

When we were all released, Caleb and Addie went back to Addie's place. Caleb stated he never wanted to return to his apartment again, and both were looking to not be alone tonight. Lora returned to her parents' house, saying she was going to sell the house she'd shared with Nessa and donate the money to a charity in Nessa's honor. She was off to find the right one.

Catherine and Walt were booked with a long list of charges. Leo said the Vancouver Police raided the chop shop the guy tailing us was associated with. There they found the car that had clipped Winnie.

Leo walked me home from the station, holding my hand. Toby shuffled ahead of us. We were all emotionally and physically tired.

The lights at my dad's newspaper were still on. "Let's go see what they're doing in there." I hoped Precious had stuck around. It had been hours since Dad texted asking me to join them.

I used my passcode to get into the front door. "Hello," I called out.

"Back here," Dad said.

We went into his office, and he and Precious were sitting at his desk. She'd pulled in another office chair. They were staring at the screen.

"What's going on here?" I asked. Whatever was on the screen had their undivided attention.

"We're building a funnel," Precious said. "Your dad is helping me with the copy in the sales funnel page." She smiled widely at me. "Come see."

This was not the same person I had seen a few days before who was contemplating their future and looking lost.

I moved to stand behind them. "What does this mean, exactly. It's a very nice... funnel ... but I don't know what that means."

Precious spun in her chair to face me. "I'm closing my business doors," she said.

"Oh no—"

"Nope," she said cutting me off. "It's a good thing. Because I'm opening my business online. I'm going big. Wide. Large."

"Yeah, I get what big means. I don't get the rest."

"I was struggling pretty hard. My company had some

national spotlight when AJ was charged with murder last year, but nothing to the caliber it had with this."

"And you weren't even working for Nessa and Lora." I felt so guilty, and I didn't know how to fix any of the mess this made.

"But what a blessing because when this all hit the fan, I got scared. Some of my more established clients were able to recognize that I was having a moment, and they didn't take on any of my bad energy. They stayed their course. But some of my not-so-established and fragile clients picked up on my bad vibes, and they scattered like rats. Some of them got ugly, too. And by the time I figured out what I was projecting and how it was affecting them, it was too late. Our relationship wasn't reparable, and their trust was gone."

"That's when I came into the picture," Dad said with a puff of his chest. "She was sitting in a pool of self-pity, trying to figure out where to go from there, when I said that ever since I've known her, she's been the type of person that only apologized when she felt it was owed. No excessive and insincere apologies from her. No sir. And I said I think why she was feeling so bad was because she's gone against who she is. That's what both of you have in common you know. You stick true to who you are."

Precious pushed back in the chair and stood, clasping her hands in front of her in excitement. "And he was right. You know what I did?"

I shook my head.

"I made an Instagram reel. I told all those people that I was sorry they were choosing to hold onto negatives, choosing to find the worst in people and that I was glad we parted ways, because as a life coach I was good, but I'm not that good. I told them happiness and fulfillment were within their grasp, but they were pushing it away. Then I wished them the best of luck and signed off."

"That's when she had a good cry," Dad said with a smile. "A good, cleansing cry. Your mother has those, like, once a month."

"It felt so good," Precious said with a contented sigh. "But then guess what happened? Sam, just guess." She was nearly bubbling over with excitement.

"Again, I got nothing. Just tell me."

She frowned. "You lack imagination."

"I've had a full day," I said, not for a second feeling any annoyance with her.

"Anyway," she said, "I started getting messages on Instagram. People asking to work with me. People from all over the world, and that's when I knew what I wanted to do. I want to help everyone. I want to offer the same chance to have a full and creative life to everyone." She pointed at the computer. "So I'm building a sales funnel and a website, and I think I'll start out with a mastermind or something where I take online students. I have so many ideas." She showed me a legal pad with writing all over it, even in the margins. "Your dad is helping me figure it all out."

I gave her the side-eye. "Are you saying that what happened with my case has actually benefited you?"

She beamed. "Crazy right. Who knew being torn apart meant getting put back together would create an even better version of myself. You know, all the signs that I wasn't satisfied with my business have been there for a while. I was all about getting involved in your cases. I wanted to work on those more than I wanted to be in my office."

"You want to be a PI?" Toby asked. He'd long ago collapsed on the couch in Dad's office. Leo was leaning against the wall with his arms crossed, watching everything unfold.

She rolled her eyes at Toby. "No, I don't want to be a PI. I wanted to grow and just didn't know how. Now I do." She grabbed me and pulled me into a hug. "I'm so thankful for you. Did I mention that?"

"I'm thankful for you, too." I hugged her back. "I'm glad you're okay."

She pushed back and looked at me. "I'm glad you're okay too. You got some ugly bruising on your forehead—"

"That was there earlier from when she played Super Mario Smash with another car," Dad said. He stood and gave me the once-over. "You said this case is closed?"

I nodded.

"And no hospital visits?"

"I know, it's crazy right?" Toby said then yawned.

"Let's all just enjoy the moment," Leo said.

None of us mentioned that I'd been shot in the back.

"And Carson?" Dad asked.

I shrugged. "He'll show back up when I need him, I guess. If everyone is good, I think I want to go upstairs and take a hot shower and crawl into bed. I may not have required a hospital stay, but I do need some meds."

Dad wrapped me in a hug. "I love you, Sammy."

"I love you too." I patted his heart.

Leo pushed away from the wall and held out a hand. I went to take it.

"Wait," Dad said. "This came for you earlier."

He held out a five-by seven manila envelope.

I took the envelope and opened the flap turning it up on its end and dumping the contents into my hand. It was a key fob and a small business card. It read: *Your new ride.*

I turned the fob over in my hand, confused.

Leo took the card. "Carson?"

"Maybe, but for some reason, I don't think so." I shrugged. "Let's go see the car. Did you see what it was, Dad?"

He shook his head. "We were in a groove. Some guy delivered the envelope, and we went back to work."

I left his office and went outside. I stood on the sidewalk outside my apartment and Dad's business. I looked at the fob. "It's a Jeep."

"There're two Jeeps down there," Toby said and pointed toward the park and the car lot where I'd played smash and roll earlier.

"There's a Jeep over there." Precious pointed across the street and up by Lark's coffee shop.

"That was stupid, to not give more information." Leo took the fob.

"I think it's that one." Dad pointed to the Jeep SUV by Lark's. "I think he said something about parking it as close as he could."

We all turned to the Jeep. I started to cross the street when Leo said. "I'm gonna hit the unlock and see which vehicle's lights blink."

A pretty silver Jeep SUV with tinted windows went *beep beep*, its lights blinking in unison.

A second later, it exploded into a massive fireball, blowing all of us backward, and shattering the windows on all the stores on the entire block.

I landed on my back and slid a couple of feet. The impact knocked the air out of me. I stared up at the stars marveling at how lovely the night sky was and how hot the flames from the explosion were.

"Everyone okay?" I called, still staring up at the sky.

"Yep," said Precious

"I'm gonna need some serious high time now," said Toby.

"Wow," said Dad.

I looked up and found him in the group. He was sitting up and looking at his office.

"Dad, you sure?"

He looked at me and tapped his heart. "Not even racing." He wagged his brows.

Leo was on his cell phone, I assumed calling it in.

I let my head come back to the pavement and looked back up at the sky.

I mean, seriously. I couldn't even get the night off?

Someone was going to pay, and finding that someone started right now.

I hope you enjoy this book. I'd love to connect and share more with you. Sign up to receive emails about and other goodies..

There, I'll share all sorts of book information. You'll be the first to know about my sales and new releases. You'll have access to giveaways, freebies, and bonus content. Think you might be interested? Give me a try. You can always leave at any time.

If so...

As football kicker Pat McAfee says: **Be a friend, tell a friend.**

You can also leave a review: Click to review

Lend it , Recommend it , Review it

XO, Kristi

MEET KRISTI ROSE

Hey! I'm Kristi. I write romances that will tug your heartstrings and laugh out loud mysteries. In all my stories you'll fall in love with the cast of characters, they'll become old, fun friends. **My one hope** is that I create stories that *satisfy any of your book cravings* and take you away from the rut of everyday life (sometimes it's a good rut).

When I'm not writing repurposing Happy Planners or drinking a London Fog (hot tea with frothy milk).

I'm the mom of 2 and a milspouse (retired). We live in the Pacific Northwest and are under-prepared if one of the volcanoes erupts.

Here are 3 things about me:

- I lived on the outskirts of an active volcano (Mt.Etna)
- A spider bit me and it laid eggs in my arm (my kids don't know that story yet)
- I grew up in Central Florida and have skied in lakes with gators.

I'd love to get to know you better. Join my Read & Relax community and then fire off an email and tell me 3 things about you!

Not ready to join? Email me below or follow me at one of the links below. Thanks for popping by!

You can connect with Kristi at any of the following:
www.kristirose.net
kristi@kristirose.net